FIC

KLA

A
Shooting
Star

A
SHOOTING
STAR

A Novel about Annie Oakley

Sheila Solomon Klass

Holiday House / New York

With love,

for Anatol Elvis Klass
— who was too young to help

and for Orlando Klass and Josephine Wolff
— who were old enough and certainly did

— S.S.K.

Copyright © 1996 by Sheila Solomon Klass
ALL RIGHTS RESERVED
Printed in the United States of America
FIRST EDITION

Library of Congress Cataloging-in-Publication Data
Klass, Sheila Solomon.
A shooting star: a novel about Annie Oakley / Sheila Solomon Klass. — 1st ed.
p. cm.
Summary: As one who prefers hunting over sewing, Annie Oakley breaks
free from conventional behavior for girls and goes on to develop her talent as a
sharpshooter and entertainer.
ISBN 0-8234-1279-2 (hardcover: alk. paper)
1. Oakley, Annie, 1860–1926 — Juvenile fiction. [1. Oakley, Annie, 1860–
1926 — Fiction. 2. Sharpshooters — Fiction. 3. Entertainers — Fiction.
4. Sex role — Fiction.] I. Title.
PZ7.K67814Sh   1996   96–16121   CIP   AC
[Fic] — dc20

18428

This is the story of me and my rifle.
But there's more to it than that.

My name is Annie Oakley, though it didn't start out that way.
I was actually named Phoebe Anne Moses.
Phew!
As far back as I can remember, I hated that name. First I got rid of the *Phoebe* part. Then I kept the *Annie*, and finally a friend gave me the *Oakley*. It took a while.
So there's even more to that.

I love guns. My gun has always been my best friend, which needs some explaining since my people are Quakers, who hate violence, and I agree with that idea one hundred percent.
I did not start hunting animals for sport or pleasure. Only because it was necessary to survive.
I would never use a gun against another person — never!

*   *   *

Why did we have a gun at all in our peaceful house?

Because we lived on the Ohio frontier — nothing but woods and fields of farmland and wild animals and game birds all around us — so a gun was a survival tool.

Even Quakers need protection from bears and wolves and dangerous snoopy strangers.

And Quakers need to eat, too.

All these peculiar things I'm going to set down here are the separate pieces of a jigsaw puzzle. Put together, they make up me.

I've been thinking on it a lot, wondering at how the odd shapes fitted right in the way they did.

How did it happen?

How come I, born Phoebe Anne Moses, grew up to be Annie Oakley, the girl with the gun — the most famous sharpshooter in the world — at a time when women were supposed to stay home sewing, cooking, and caring for their families?

How come?

1

SOME FOLKS SAY 13 is an unlucky number.

I was born on August 13, 1860; so whenever hard times knocked me down, I used to blame old unlucky 13 as I picked myself up and brushed myself off. I'd think to myself — *If only* — it'd all be different *if only* my birthdate were 12 or 14. . . .

If only doesn't do a whit of good. Especially about birthdates. *If only* I'd been born that very same August on 12 or 14, why, I'd be somebody else.

Anyway, my hard times weren't really 13's fault, because I had good times, too. How could I account for all those happy times? All those family times, funny times, loving times?

The whole first six years of my life on the Ohio prairie.

That's where I began. I'm the fifth of seven children born to Jacob Moses, a farmer, and his wife, Susan, who'd moved west from Pennsylvania.

First there was Lydia, Mary Jane, Elizabeth, and Sarah Ellen; next came you-know-who; then my brother, John, and baby Hulda.

My parents were Quakers, "plain people." Since there were no other Quakers living out West near us,

Ma and Pa couldn't go to Meeting, but both of them were deeply religious. They believed each person has to pay attention to his own inner life and to God. That was how I was raised.

We children lived outdoors, gloriously, three seasons of the year.

During the summer we went berrying. There were red haws and strawberries, blackberrries, and raspberries growing wild in the fields. We picked and I ate, we picked and I ate. I was always hungry for wild fruit.

"You eat more'n you pick, Annie," Pa said to me once, when I was real small.

I went off and sat on a rock and thought about it awhile till I figured out that wasn't possible, and I came back and told him, "Pa, that can't be. No un can eat more berries 'n she picks. They ain't there in the basket to eat."

He laughed and said he was only teasing. I loved the way Pa teased me. He was a man who liked to laugh.

Not Ma. She was always right serious. She said she was a doer and not much of a talker, and she spoke true. She worked hard: cooking, cleaning, sewing, and farming, looking after all of us and taking care of us.

Ma never believed in wasting anything, least of all *time*. Funning wasted time.

From before sunup they both labored. Still, Pa could always find a minute for a riddle or a story or just good talk.

Nights by the fireside, after he'd given the older girls their lessons, he'd sit with us younger children and tell us wonderful tales about knights and dragons or fairies and elves, and even, sometimes — though Ma feared he'd frighten us — he'd tell a spooky story about ghosts and monsters.

His favorite talking subject was history — true things that really happened long long ago.

But mostly he'd talk about the terrible war going on right then between the North and the South. Pa was against slavery like many of the folks in Ohio, but plenty of others were for it. Ohio was divided just like the rest of the country. "Split," Pa said, "and suffering."

He and I were real good friends. Talking times in the firelight were learning times, happy times, and old 13 gave them to me.

We children hoed and weeded in the garden, then helped to harvest pumpkins and squash and onions and other vegetables. We lent our hands to building and mending fences. Sometimes we'd set search for apples blown down from trees and we'd track them down in the grass like detectives hunting for jewels. They looked like jewels, all rosy and yellow and green.

Even a small child like me could catch crawfish in the creek. And I did.

In the autumn we collected nuts from the trees growing all around; we had hazelnuts and hickories and butternuts and black walnuts raining down right near our cabin. I didn't eat near as many nuts as berries; shelling nuts was too much work.

So we ran about and played and fished and I

thought that was the way life was always going to be.

Free and happy.

Till a freak early fall blizzard came along when I was six.

One dark, gloomy October afternoon, Pa hitched up the wagon to go to town and buy supplies. Ma, looking up at the heavy clouds, said, "Best not go. A storm is brewing."

Pa heard her out, then studied the sky. He considered himself a good judge of weather. "That storm is way to the east," he decided. "I'll be back long before anything starts up here. We'll need the provisions if we get snowed in. You're almost clear out of flour."

"Please," Ma begged. "Don't go."

Pa was positive he was right, so he set off.

That storm came rushing in so fast we barely got our livestock indoors. First there were howling winds, then heavy wet snow blew in through small cracks in our cabin. We sat waiting and waiting for Pa till well into the night. Ma was worried sick; she forgot to send me to bed, so I was there when the wagon finally did come back in the early morning. It came back only because the horse knew the way.

Pa was lying in the seat, stiff as a scarecrow, half froze. Ma and my big sisters gently carried him in and laid him down on a quilt near the fire. They tried their best to warm him, to get him to speak, to drink some warm soup, to open his eyes — but he was too far gone.

I had one look at his face when he was lying there on our hearth under a mound of bedding. It didn't look like Pa's face. It looked like a white mask — a terrible, twisted mask of some stranger.

I began to sob and Ma sent me out.

They moved him onto the bed and for a few months he just lay that way near the fire, coughing and not knowing any of us — and then in midwinter he died.

I was very young. I couldn't understand what happened. I only understood that there was a terrible hole in the world now that Pa was gone. A hole so big and deep and dark it scared me when I closed my eyes at night, and I screamed and kicked something fierce.

Ma took to burning the kerosene lantern till morning so's I could sleep.

It was costly, but I always remember she kept that light on for me.

2

SUDDENLY, we were very poor.

Ma was left alone to look after all of us.

We tried to help. We gathered and fished and harvested just as before, working harder and harder at it. I stopped eating berries; I just picked and put every single one in the basket. Even the squidgy ones, 'cause they're good enough in jam and pies.

Whatever Ma could do even with us helping was not enough.

Then she married a neighbor, Dan Brumbaugh, who was kind to us, but I missed Pa. Dan Brumbaugh was poor, too. He had an acre of land and a cabin we moved into. Soon Ma was pregnant, and then my baby sister Emily was born.

When Emily was only five months old, Dan Brumbaugh died. We had hardly got used to him, and he was gone.

By the time I was eight years old I knew that things were desperate, and I made up my mind to do my best to help.

What was my best, way out there on the frontier?

Though I'd longed to go to school, there was no

schoolhouse in our tiny village. All North Star had was one store, a church, and a smithy, with families like us scattered all around.

Ma tried after Pa's death to give us some lessons: reading, writing, and sums.

She was a stern schoolmistress.

And I was her worst pupil. I wanted to learn, but whatever I studied flitted right out of my head. I couldn't catch on to reading and writing no matter what. I tried my best.

"I don't understand," Ma would say. "A girl like you with a good head, a quick sharp mind, should have no trouble with reading."

Then the lessons stopped. Ma simply could not provide and care for us and teach us, too. She was plain tuckered out.

So Mother Nature became my teacher. Roaming about outdoors all day in the woods and fields, I studied the patterns of the wildlife. I became a scout. I spied on the wild birds: the quail when they came to feed, the wild ducks, and the grouse. I memorized their habits.

Enough puzzling about the birds and small animals led me to figure something out in my head.

I pieced together some homemade traps, once I knew just where to go to set them. It's a wonder that I ever caught anything in those crude devices, but once in a while they worked!

Rabbits sometimes hopped into my twisted snares;

and grouse and quail, greedy for the kernels of corn I used for bait, fell into the cornstalk traps buried under branches.

I felt mighty smart each time I caught something. Just the way Pa said Columbus must have felt when he discovered America and began to yell, "Land ho!"

"Turkey ho!" I'd yell, hopping around on one foot happily till my sisters and brother all came running to see. "Turkey ho ho ho!"

We'd have a little turkey hop celebrating meat for dinner!

Ma was mighty pleased with me and grateful when I brought home a game bird or animal I'd trapped, and, of course, my sisters and brother were delighted.

So I helped once in a while to fill our bellies. But it didn't happen often enough to matter much. We were still struggling. We had no income.

I used to walk alone in the woods and ask out loud, "How else can I help? What else can I do?"

Only the birds and the raccoons and other small animals and the tall trees heard me, and none of them had an answer.

Then one day an idea flashed into my head.

Where do ideas come from? I don't know, but I believe if you worry a problem long enough, your mind gets tired of it and answers it just to get rid of it.

This particular day my brother, John, who was almost six, and I were alone in the cabin. Ma had gotten the job of district nurse — which earned her one dollar twenty-five cents a week — but she had to travel out to care for the sick. The younger children were left with neighbors, my older sisters had chores, and that's how I came to be sitting on that bench with John.

He and I were huddled near the hearth trying to stay warm from the banked fire. We were both a little hungry. Seems we were always a little cold and a little hungry.

I spotted a rabbit outside our window. "Look at that rabbit, John," I said. "He's a nice fat young fellow." In my head I could already see him and smell him all juicy and tender in a stew. I could already taste him.

John rubbed his belly and grinned. He had rabbit stew simmering in his head, too.

My eyes lit on my father's gun resting on pegs on the wall. The barrel was dull with dust.

A boldness came into me.

"That rabbit probably got so fat eating *our* cabbages in *our* garden," I grumbled. "Now it's *his* turn to pay us back."

All of a sudden, I was up and climbing onto a stool. "Hold my feet steady, Johnny boy," I said, and I reached up for that rifle. It was bigger than me and mighty heavy, but I held on tight and I lugged it down.

"What you gonna do, Annie?" John asked. He looked real scared.

"Watch and see. I'm gonna get us the rabbit for dinner. Will you help me?"

"But we're not supposed to *ever, ever* —"

"*Shh*, Johnny. Don't you want rabbit stew?"

He bounced his head, yes, yes, yes.

I had never touched a gun before. I was scared, too, don't think I wasn't. Our family were people of peace. The only reason Pa ever got that gun to begin with was that we lived in a dangerous world.

I had to load it. I'd watched my father load it many times, and he used to let me help by holding the bag of bullets or the ramrod, the stick that shoves the bullet down. I was just going to copy exactly what he did.

But Pa had never worked with a dirty gun. "Clean tools work best," he'd always said, and I heard it in my head right then.

First, I got a cloth and dusted and rubbed that gun till the long blue barrel was shiny again. Then I polished the stock till its wood gleamed. I put the cloth on the ramrod and shoved it into the barrel, working it around to get the grit out of the inside.

"Be careful, Annie," John worried.

"There's nothing in it yet," I said.

Going to the cupboard, I fetched the little deerskin bag of bullets and handed it to John. "You're the holder. You get to hold the bullets," I told him. "That's what I used to do for Pa. He said the holder had the second most important job."

John took the bag very carefully, dangling it by its drawstrings, keeping it away from himself as if it were a poisonous spider. He was sitting straight up, looking proud, his brown eyes shining but his face still scared.

"Those bullets can't hurt you, Johnny. They're just pieces of lead. I've got to put the powder in first."

John turned his head to look out the window. "The rabbit's gone," he noted sadly.

"We'll get the gun all ready and wait for him or his friends to come back." I spoke my plans out loud to keep up his spirits. Inside, I was really hoping.

I fetched the cow horn filled with gunpowder and tried to measure the powder same as Pa did, one capful using the horn's metal cap.

Level or heaping? I wondered.

Here, I had a serious problem.

Closing my eyes, I did my best to remember, but it had been more than two years.

Well, I couldn't remember.

Level might be too little to send a fast bullet. I decided to leave it all up to chance.

"You're heaping," I said to Johnny, "and I'm level." I made a fist and began. "Eenie, meenie, minie, mo . . ." It ended up on Johnny.

Heaping! Real heaping to overflowing, I decided. Like sugar in a cake.

I figured if you put in extra sugar, what harm did it do? It only made the cake sweeter.

I set the rifle on the floor, butt down, and carefully poured the thin stream of powder into the barrel. I jiggled the gun a little to make sure all the powder was down. I jiggled it again and again.

"Hand me a bullet, John," I commanded.

Bravely, he took one out and gave it to me.

I pushed that bullet down the barrel with the ram-rod, and I pressed hard a score of times, making sure it was way down where it belonged.

"Ready!" I said. "Let's not waste time in here. Let's go find us our dinner."

I was surprised at how big and heavy the gun was when I tried to lift it onto my shoulder. I could barely walk with it resting there, and I had to take each step real slow and careful.

Out we went into the pasture, and we crept behind some bushes. "You stay here, John," I whispered. "I'll move downways a little."

"Why, Annie?"

"It was a rule Pa had — never to keep anyone near him when he was shooting."

Well, we settled down real quiet to wait.

I couldn't rightly say if it was the same rabbit or his twin brother, but when I was almost ready to give up and my eyes were stinging with tears at disappointing Johnny and disobeying Ma for nothing — she would see the shiny gun and know I'd touched it — guess who came along? Mr. Rabbit Stew. He was hopping, then snuffling; hopping, then snuffling.

I readied the rifle and squinted down the barrel through the sight, and when I saw him perfectly, just as he hopped I pulled the trigger.

The explosion knocked me down so hard, I squinched my eyes tight shut and decided I was dead.

"Oh Lord," I prayed, "make Ma find that rabbit and cook him for dinner tonight even if I am dead."

My ears were ringing and through the ringing I heard John calling from far off.

"Annie, Annie are you hurt?"

Well, I figured I wasn't dead.

I opened my eyes. "Too much gunpowder," I said. "Don't work at all like sugar in a cake. Should have been level, not heaping."

"Your face is all smudgy." John laughed with relief.

"Did I get him?"

"Let's go see." John helped me up. I left the empty gun lying there for a minute and ran with him.

I had got that rabbit. Shot clean through the head!

"Rabbit — ho!" I screamed, and Johnny with me. "Rabbit ho! Rabbit ho!" But there was no one nearby to hear us.

So Johnny and I made up a single-file parade. He led the way, his arm stretched out and hand held way up high in front, carrying the rabbit by its ears, while I wobbled along behind him, weaving this way and that with the gun. Once back inside, we could hardly bear to wait for Ma.

How come she's taking so long? we wondered.

We'll wait till she gets inside, we agreed; then we'll surprise her.

Wasn't she ever going to get home?

Every other minute one of us ran to unlock the front door and peek out at the road.

Had something happened to her?

The two of us were standing there together in the doorway as the wagon rolled in sight.

Johnny couldn't wait. "Ma! Ma! Guess what?" he shouted, soon as the wagon jolted to a stop. He was dancing with joy. "You'll never guess! Annie shot us a big rabbit."

3

MA CLIMBED DOWN from the wagon.

She did not answer Johnny. Nor did she call out, "Rabbit ho!" or lift her hand to wave or even look up at us.

Slowly, she moved up the path, her nurse's bag in her hand, her face grave with the plain brown bonnet.

Her first words were severe. "Thee are not allowed to touch the gun, Phoebe Anne." Ma always spoke in the old Quaker way and *always* insisted on using my detested name.

"I know how," I said, grinning like a fool.

She stood there, silent, studying me.

"I'm careful. I learned how from Pa."

Her careworn face remained serious.

"I wanted to give us rabbit stew for dinner. I shot him clean in the head. See?"

Ma came close and examined my catch and then shook her head. "The first time thee used a gun. It's a wonder. Perhaps Providence has given thee a special talent, child." She stopped. "A queer one, for it is misplaced in a girl."

She turned away, then back, and she bent over and

grazed my forehead with her lips. I touched the spot with wonder many times afterward. To this day I can put my finger exactly where that kiss rested.

"We'd best fix dinner now," was all she said.

Well, that was the best rabbit stew ever eaten in the whole state of Ohio!

Ma served the stew with fresh vegetables from the garden, and there was enough good gravy for all. For dessert, she'd baked two blackberry pies.

If I shut my eyes right now, I can still taste each dish in that feast: the soft, plump chunks of rabbit with wild mushrooms cooked slowly in butter and herbs, the golden turnips and runner beans, the white mounds of mashed potatoes with rivers of gravy spilling over them. And then the pies with spurts of blackberry juice peeking up through the fork holes in perfect fluted crusts.

During the next two years — when my own life was terrible and I was far from home and cut off from family — I would think of that evening around the table, my sisters and my brother and Ma and me all close together; safe, happy faces in the firelight.

In the privacy of my mind, in the darkness I would repeat, *Rabbit ho! Rabbit ho!* And then I would cry myself to sleep.

Ma was right. I had a special talent.

It wasn't the one she would've chosen for me, but it was mine, all mine.

*   *   *

It was natural for me to begin to use it. But each time I shot a bird or an animal, Ma made a terrible fuss, going on and on about how I must not shoot again. Traps were all right, but shooting was *not* for womenfolk.

I was stubborn, she scolded. Stubbornness was evil, a weakness of character. I would have to fight against that stubbornness.

Each time, she made me feel real bad. Because, secretly, I was proud of my shooting. I did it so well.

Then, before we'd worked things out between us, two terrible events happened in a row.

First, my dear sister, Mary Jane, caught a chill and took sick and just got sicker and sicker. I loved her so. She was tall and thin and graceful, and she'd sing pretty songs to us. I couldn't believe it when she died. Pa then Dan Brumbaugh and now Mary Jane. It was too much to understand.

Next, I got sent away.

One afternoon, a woman who'd come by right after Pa died came to visit Ma again. After they'd been sitting and talking awhile, Ma called for me to come in.

"This is Mrs. Crawford Eddington," Ma said.

The lady had a kind face. "How do you do, Phoebe Anne?"

"Ma'am," I said politely.

"Mrs. Eddington is in charge of the county farm," Ma said.

A coldness clutched at my heart. The county farm, about forty miles away, was the poorhouse for folks no one wanted. Everyone called it the infirmary. Old people who couldn't take care of themselves, orphans, and lunatics lived in the infirmary. When no one wanted you, that was where you ended up.

"I need a helper," Mrs. Eddington said. "Your mother and I think you might be better off with me."

I hid my face in my hands.

"Your mother says you would like to go to school," she continued. "Would you? Would you like to learn to read and write?"

"Oh, yes."

"Well, I am looking for a smart, willing girl to help me with the small children and do some sewing. In exchange for your help, I will teach you to sew and see that you get schooling. I try to give our girls a good home."

"Oh no," I said. "I already have a good home." I looked to Ma frantically.

She had clasped her hands and closed her eyes.

"Think about it," Mrs. Eddington said, rising to go. "Both of you. It's a big decision. I will be by this way next Tuesday afternoon and you can tell me what you've decided. If you're coming, Phoebe Anne —"

She saw the frown on my forehead at the sound of that hated name, so she looked at Ma inquiringly.

"The child dislikes her name," Ma said wearily. "It's foolishness."

"What do you want to be called?"

"Annie," I said.

"Very well — Annie. At the county farm you may be called Annie if you prefer."

I looked to Ma. She didn't object.

Did she really want me to go?

I stared at her steadily, praying, wishing that she'd speak.

"If you decide to come stay with me," Mrs. Eddington continued, "have your things ready."

And she went away.

Once she'd gone, I ran to Ma and grabbed her around the waist and held on and begged, "Don't send me so far away. I'll work hard here. I don't eat a single berry anymore when I'm picking. And now that I can shoot —"

"I cannot help it, child."

"Please, Ma. Oh, please —"

"Thee must go."

"I don't want to live in the poorhouse! I beg of you, Ma."

"I cannot manage," she said firmly, removing my arms. "The three younger children will board with neighbors and thee must go away for a while. Not for too long, I promise."

"I can't bear it," I said, weeping.

"Mrs. Eddington is a good woman. She will treat thee kindly."

"That doesn't matter. I want to be here with my family. First I lost Pa, then Mary Jane. I don't want to lose everyone!"

"Phoebe Anne, thee *must* go."

I knew that tone. There was iron in it. There was no use begging.

When I told John that I was going away, he cried and held on to me. "I want to go with you," he sobbed. "I'll never see you again."

"Uh-huh. I'll come back," I said. "We'll get us a bunch of rabbits. And quail and wild turkeys. You'll see."

That didn't stop his crying.

"And I'll teach you to shoot —"

He quieted down and began rubbing his eyes with his fists. "Promise?"

I nodded.

"Take the gun with you, Annie —"

"I can't. Ma would never let me."

He ran to the cupboard and got the little deerskin bag with bullets. "Then take this for good luck. No one else will need it till you come back. Pa's gun is *yourn* now."

"I will take the shot bag, Johnny." Now I was the one nearly crying. "As a keepsake. To remind me of our rabbit."

I was ready early in my best dress, a blue gingham Ma had made me, my few clothes packed in a box and the shot bag well hidden under them.

Just before Mrs. Eddington came back, Ma said quietly, "I've tucked some lengths of fine pink silk I saved in the box. Sew something pretty, child."

That silk was part of Ma's trousseau carried from the East on a wagon and kept wrapped in tissue in her old wooden trunk. I'd admired it many times. I guess in her way she was telling me how sorry she was. But she never spoke it outright.

I waited, hoping, till the very last minute, but all I got as her blessing was the length of pink silk.

That day I said goodbye not only to my family but to the outdoors: to the green fields and forests and the brook, to the blue of the daytime sky lit by its golden sun and the black of the nighttime sky with all its glowing stars and planets, and to all the wildlife that I loved.

I said goodbye to freedom.

4

"AH, THE INFIRMARY." Mrs. Eddington yawned with tiredness. "Home at last, child."

Maybe for her, but not for me!

It was nightfall and we'd come a very long way.

This *home* was a big, three-story brick building with great wooden doors. It loomed right at the edge of the road. Like the fortresses in Pa's stories — with dungeons in them. The very size of it made me tremble. We had no such buildings on the prairie.

Climbing out of the wagon, I carried my box inside and up the stairs into a long, dim room filled with beds placed one next to the other, where all the poorhouse children slept.

When I first came in, I didn't see anyone, but I heard odd noises — the sound of pebbles scattering on wood. I followed the sound and saw a girl sitting cross-legged on the floor between the beds, hidden, tossing jackstones as she played a game of dibs.

I loved that game. "Hello," I said. "I'm Annie."

She caught up all her pebbles in her fist and stopped playing, and her eyes opened very wide as she smiled a little scared smile, but she didn't say a single word.

Or make a sound. Nothing at all. Instead, she put her forefinger over her lips to signal silence. A secret?

I thought, *Maybe she can't talk*. I'd heard Mrs. Eddington telling Ma there were people in the poorhouse like that. Some went around muttering the same thing over and over. One old farm woman said "Porridge and pork chops" all the time. Others were silent as ghosts.

"Can I play?" I asked.

She nodded and I sat down on the floor across from her. Her thin face and her dark eyes and the graceful way she moved her hands reminded me of my poor dead sister Mary Jane.

She was amazing with those jackstones, her hands were so nimble and fast. We had a real good game, but she never said a word out loud.

Then, that lonely first night, as I lay awake in the dark for a long miserable time, I felt a hand reach over and touch my elbow, and I heard a whisper. "I'm glad you're here, Annie. I'm Sally Jones. How old are you?"

I could barely hear her.

"Going on nine."

"I'm near to eleven . . . but I'm not sure of my birthdate."

I'd never heard of such a thing. "How come?"

"I'll tell you when I know you better. When we're true friends." Her voice grew even softer. "I bet you thought I couldn't talk."

"That *is* what I thought."

"I try not to talk when any of the others are around," she whispered. "They call me Silent Sally."

"But why?"

"Because — because — it's safer. They're bullies. And I'm not strong. I can't fight. You'll see."

It was all very strange, but knowing that there was a friend lying a-side me helped me fall asleep at last.

Next morning when I woke, she was standing by her bed in her long white nightgown, smiling at me. I was glad she was there.

Sally was tall and very skinny but graceful as could be, with a doll face, black eyes fringed with thick black lashes, soft ivory-colored skin, and silky long black hair worn in a tight braid down her back. She was gentle as a baby deer.

The bed on the other side of me was empty.

"That's Emmeline Sue's bed, but she broke her leg climbing out the window trying to run away from here. So she's in the sickroom," Sally told me. She stopped, and then she said a funny thing. "Beware of Emmeline Sue." And she rolled her eyes.

I couldn't get her to tell me any more. But each day I'd look at that empty bed nervously.

Beware is a scary word.

Since it was summer and there was no school, I sat all day by a window in the sewing room learning how to make tiny stitches neat and tight in straight rows. Very quickly I was mending torn clothes, then sewing shifts and nightgowns.

There was so much to do, there wasn't even time to

look out the window and notice the glorious summer outside.

Mrs. Eddington *was* kind and she liked me. "Annie" was what she called me, never once Phoebe Anne. She even began to teach me fancy stitching, smocking, and fagoting.

"Sewing is a useful and respectable trade," she said. "You will make an excellent seamstress one day."

She repeated it whenever I did a creditable job of stitching, because she was pleased at this fine future she saw for me.

I suffered at the idea of a life locked indoors all day every day.

When I wasn't sewing, those first weeks, I was kept busy either helping with the small children or cleaning, emptying chamber pots or doing kitchen work. The infirmary was large and full of unpleasant chores and we children got to do many of them.

Life was just about as hard and empty as it could be. Except for Sally.

Soon she and I were best friends. If either of us got an apple or an orange, or when she got a cinnamon stick for sitting up very late with a croupy child, or if I got some horehound drops from Mrs. Eddington for special sewing — we shared. We ate half as much each, but it was doubly sweet. Like a party.

Since the poorhouse was Sally's longtime home, she knew a secret hideout, a storeroom, where we could sit and talk. A dusty place but private.

Every chance we got, we slipped away. We acted

out fairy tales that Pa had told: *Rapunzel* and *Hansel and Gretel* and *Rumpelstiltskin.* We made up spooky ghost stories or fantastic tales of princes and dragons and beautiful princesses who were always rescued just in time.

Sally taught me some of her tricks with jackstones, but I never got to be as good at dibs as she was. She was a whiz. I told her how I could shoot a rifle and I showed her my precious shot bag. "Ma says I have a talent," I said. "A shooting talent."

"You're lucky," she admired. "A talent is a special thing."

"You have one with jackstones, Sally," I said, and she smiled so sweetly. I don't think anyone had ever said anything nice to her before.

One morning the bed next to me was all mussed up, and from the confusion of blankets and sheets hanging all over, out stomped Emmeline, barefooted.

When she first caught sight of me, she walked around my bed and came sniffing all around me the way a dog does. Then she went around me once again, eyeing, her chin in her hand like she was thinking.

She was a chunky girl. Her curly yellow hair was in a big tangle, as if it had never met a comb, and on her left cheek were four half-moons dug in under the eye — fingernail scars. She had a turned-up nose and more freckles than a trout.

"You — what's your name?" she asked.

"Annie."

"Annie what?"

I didn't care to tell. So I turned my back and pretended I was busy smoothing my bedclothes and hadn't heard the question.

"Hey!" She pulled at my sleeve. "Hey, you. Ain't you got no manners? You don't turn your back on Emmeline Sue Smathers."

I pulled away to free myself and heard my sleeve tear.

She let go. "So?" She stood waiting.

I kept quiet.

Again, "Annie what?" Then she stamped her foot, hard. "You deaf? Annie what . . . Annie what . . . Annie what?"

"Annie Moses." I tried my best to mumble.

"Moses?" Emmeline Sue began to laugh and laugh. "No wonder you didn't want to say. What a name! Moses!"

The other girls looked at her.

She was close to me, so close I could hear her loud breathing, and she leaned the top half of her body back a bit and pointed at me. "Moses-Poses!" she shrieked. "Moses-Poses."

First, one of them laughed, and then a couple more of them joined in and picked up the hateful rhyme. They came over to stand real close to me, their spiteful mouths picking it up and saying it over and over. "Moses-Poses! Moses-Poses!"

It went on a long time till I thought I would just die

there if they didn't leave off. Finally they got tired of chanting it, and they wandered off.

Sally had just kept quiet and crouched on her bed out of their way through it all. I didn't blame her. What could she do?

Later, she did try to comfort me. "It's not your name that's at fault. Emmeline would go after you no matter what you were called."

"It don't matter. I hate my name. Always have."

Emmeline Sue Smathers somehow could always figure out what would torture a person the most. I believe there are cruel people who are especially good at that kind of figuring.

She and her mean friends took my name and set it in a jingle, and they chanted it at me every chance they could.

> Moses-Poses
> Moses-Poses
> No one knows
> Where she gets her clothes-es.

That ugly chorus echoed in my ears, morning to night, wherever I went in the poorhouse, as if the green walls themselves were whispering it and mocking me.

One very rainy Sunday, Emmeline Sue was on the warpath. All morning she and her buddies had been humming or singing "Moses-Poses." I went about holding my ears.

In my pocket I had hidden a big surprise for Sally, but I didn't dare give it.

After lunch, Sally signaled me to follow her quick, and once away we ran to our hideout, on the top floor, the furniture storeroom filled with beds and mattresses and chairs covered by sheets.

It was snug and safe in there. And dusty.

As we huddled together, I told Sally about my family, all about Pa dying, and then about Mary Jane and everything.

She was quiet a long time after I finished.

"I never had a family," she said. "I've lived here always. I was just dropped off on the front steps here like a bag of laundry early one morning. Mrs. Eddington named me Sally Jones. She says she reckons I should think of her as my mother — and she is nice — but you can't *think* a mother, can you, Annie?"

I felt so sad, I hugged her. "No," I said. "But I will make you my friend-sister. Wherever I go and whatever happens to me, I will always think of you and talk to you in my head. I promise, every single day. And even if you can't hear me, you'll know that somewhere a friend-sister is talking to you."

"And I will do the same," she promised, smiling the shiest smile. "I never had a real friend or a sister before."

Nor had Sally ever had a present from anyone that

was made especially for her. Not even a corncob doll when she was small.

Well, she was too big now for a doll, but I had secretly taken some of Ma's pink silk and hemmed her a scarf. I'd cross-stitched a pattern of red roses along its border. I would have embroidered her name on it, except I was fearful I wouldn't get the letters facing right.

I gave it to her now.

"I love this scarf more than anything in the world," she said. "I can't wear it, and I'll keep it hidden from Emmeline Sue and the other hateful girls. I'll sleep with it under my pillow." She ran her hand over it. "It's so soft and pretty, Annie.

"One day I'll wear it," she promised me. "One special day."

Outside our hiding place we heard shoes scuffling and then Emmeline's nasty voice calling to the others. "I wonder where they are, the two dummies. The one that talks and the one that don't. They ain't smart enough to get away from us."

But we were.

Emmeline jiggled the bolted door. "Locked," she grumbled. "They can't be in there."

We sat still, hands held tight over our mouths, sealing in our laughter and the sneezes caused by the dust.

Two good friends.

Together.

Safe!

5

"SCHOOL STARTS TODAY," Mrs. Eddington said to me one morning. "You still want to go?"

"More than anything."

"Very well. You may go this morning and every day that I can spare you."

"Thank you." I grinned.

"That's the first time since you came here that I've seen such a happy face," she said, pleased. "One thing, Annie. I offered you schooling as a condition for coming here, but school is a great privilege. I cannot offer it to everyone. Don't make a great fuss about going. Keep it to yourself."

"Yes, ma'am," I promised.

The only one I told was Sally, and I warned her that it had to be kept secret. "Don't let on to anyone, or they'll just tease and make trouble."

"I won't," she promised. "Maybe what you learn you can pass on to me. I know my letters, and I can read some."

"We'll teach each other."

Every day I helped with morning washup and breakfasts and then I waited, holding my breath. Some days yes and other days no. I would get to go to school whenever Mrs. Eddington could spare me, and I loved it.

I was almost nine years old, yet all I knew was the alphabet. I began to try to read in the *McGuffey Eclectic Primer* and to trace the letters in the "Script Exercises" on my slate.

Mr. and Mrs. Ebenezer Aspinwall-Jones together ran the school. He taught the boys and she taught the girls. Both of them were real tall, large people. With red hair. Almost giants.

Maybe their tallness was why they became teachers. Because from the front of the schoolroom, they could see everything that went on and every single child, and we never lost sight of them for a minute, either. You couldn't do mischief if you wanted to in their school.

Anyway, I didn't want to. I wanted to learn.

They were very strict but fair. "We are missionaries," Mrs. Aspinwall-Jones told us, "and our mission in life is to educate you prairie children."

One afternoon the schoolmistress kept me after school to talk to me. "Annie, you have a good head, but you have problems learning. I don't know what causes them. If you could attend every day, you would do much better."

Almost the exact words Ma had said to me when we had done lessons at home. A good head, a keen mind, but learning problems. Why? Where did the problems come from?

"Practice is what does it, Annie," the schoolmistress encouraged me.

"I'll do my best, Ma'am," I promised. "Thank you for your help."

Ma would've said, "Providence has not given thee a learning talent, but thee needst be grateful for other blessings."

How homesick I was for my mother's Quaker speech.

I wanted urgently to ask a favor of my teacher, but I held back awhile because I was scared. It was a very big favor, and I didn't want her to say no.

Finally, one recess time when all the other students were outdoors, I pinched my fingers tight into fists and I waited at her desk and I spoke up. "Ma'am, the girl in the next bed to me has taught herself her letters and can already read some. She would like to learn more but has no copybook or reader. Is there a spare copybook and a reader she might use?"

Mrs. Aspinwall-Jones shook her head as if she had water in her ears. "She has taught herself?"

I nodded. "She is very quick to learn."

"Extraordinary. Of course you two may work together and help each other." She found a copybook for Sally to write in, and she lent me a *McGuffey Eclectic Reader* to take home. The cover was wrinkled and water damaged, but inside it was perfect, and there were dozens of new and wonderful stories and poems.

Months passed. I couldn't be in school every day. Many days I was needed to sew or help with the poorhouse children: to dress, to wash, to lace, to comb them.

And to nurse them, too.

In the spring we had a spell of sickness in the infirmary, first scarlet fever, then mumps. I escaped the scarlet fever and helped care for the others, but then I caught mumps and was very swollen and hot and sick for more than a week.

When I'd recovered, Mrs. Eddington said, "Now Annie, you'll have to help in the sickroom with the mumps patients."

"I'm afraid," I told her truthfully. "I couldn't bear to catch it again."

"You won't," she said cheerfully. "Mumps is a one-time disease."

And she had told me true. I did help out in the sickroom — boy, was Emmeline Sue ugly when she got it. Not only did she look liked a speckled trout, but she almost turned into one! She lost her voice for a whole week.

I stayed well.

But I missed many school days. Still, on the days I got to go, I learned whatever Mrs. Aspinwall-Jones taught.

Sally and I did lessons when we could sneak off. She was so fast, she jumped way ahead of me in the reading. She could almost always help me figure out hard words.

Suddenly — in school — there was big excitement. Elocution Night was on hand. Parents and important folks from town were coming to hear students read or recite or answer questions. Our class was going to "do" poetry.

Well, I had no folks nearby, and I couldn't go out at night anyway. I was miserable sad about it because I loved poems. It would have been so much fun to recite my favorite.

"Let's each memorize a poem," Sally suggested. "Then we'll dress up and pretend we're there — and recite for each other."

It was a dilly of an idea.

Each of us chose a poem then worked on memorizing it privately. We gave ourselves a week. On Saturday, after chores, we sneaked off for our own private Elocution Afternoon.

Sally insisted I go first. I was wearing the same dress I had left home in, my blue gingham with three pearly buttons in a row under the neck. My thick brown hair was loose down my back, and when I looked in the mirror my gray-blue eyes were sparkling with excitement.

Standing straight and proud, mindful of all the hints Mrs. Aspinwall-Jones had given my classmates, I looked right out at the audience and began.

My Mother

(author anonymous)

Hark! my mother's voice I hear,
Sweet that voice is to my ear;

Ever soft, it seems to tell,
Dearest child I love thee well.

Love me, mother? Yes, I know
None can love so well as thou.
Was it not upon thy breast
I was taught to sleep and rest?

Didst thou not, in hours of pain
Lull this head to ease again?
With the music of thy voice,
Bid my little heart rejoice?

Ever gentle, meek, and mild,
Thou didst nurse thy fretful child
Teach these little feet the road
Leading on to heaven and God.

What return then can I make?
This fond heart, dear mother, take;
Thine it is, in word and thought,
Thine by constant kindness bought.

"Curtsy," Sally prompted, and she clapped her hands as I bobbed up and down. "That was wonderful." She shook my hand like the teacher would. "You knew it perfectly. You're really smart, Annie."

Then she stood up, proud and tall. On her shoulders she'd draped the pink scarf with the red roses I'd sewed her. And when she began to recite her poem, I could see her and hear every remarkable thing happening as if I were really there.

Ballad of the Tempest
by James T. Fields

We were crowded in the cabin;
　　Not a soul would dare to sleep, —
It was midnight on the waters,
　　And a storm was on the deep.

'Tis a fearful thing in winter
　　To be shattered by the blast
And to hear the rattling trumpet
　　Thunder, "Cut away the mast!"

So we shuddered there in silence —
　　For the stoutest held his breath,
While the hungry sea was roaring
　　And the breakers talked with death.

As thus we sat in darkness,
　　Each one busy in his prayers,
"We are lost!" the captain shouted,
　　As he staggered down the stairs.

But his little daughter whispered,
　　As she took his icy hand,
"Isn't God upon the ocean,
　　Just the same as on the land?"

Then we kissed the little maiden,
　　And we spoke in better cheer;
And we anchored safe in harbor
　　When the morn was shining clear.

It was my turn to clap my hands hard.

Sally curtsied to the left and to the right and then to me in the middle. I had to wipe tears from my eyes. Then we enjoyed refreshments — gingersnaps saved from dinner and apples. Our Elocution Afternoon was a big success, the happiest time we'd spent in the infirmary.

That happiness was short lived.

The very next morning while I was in school, Emmeline Sue came hurrying into the infants' room where Sally was helping diaper the babies, and she said, "Mrs. Eddington wants Moses-Poses in a rush, and she's in big trouble if she don't come."

Then she waited.

Sally paid her no mind and went on diapering.

"I heard Mrs. Eddington say Moses-Poses is gonna be dismissed and sent away. Come on, dummy. Where is she?"

Sally shrugged her shoulders to show she didn't know.

Emmeline Sue stood fast, tapping her foot and waiting, full of spite. "Then you better say goodbye to Moses-Poses."

Sally panicked.

"Did Mrs. Eddington r-r-really s-s-say that?"

"May I break my other leg if she didn't."

"Well — Annie's in sc — sc —"

Poor Sally. She didn't want me to be dismissed. She wanted so much to save me.

"Sc —? School?" Once Emmeline Sue figured it out, she and her friends were mad that I had that privilege.

It wasn't that they wanted to go to school. They just didn't want me to go.

By the time I returned from school, they had new rhymes to use to torture me.

> Moses-Poses
> Goes to school
> Moses-Poses
> Is a fool.
>
> Moses-Poses
> Can't even think
> Moses-Poses
> Really stinks.

Sally felt real terrible about telling, though I told her it wasn't her fault.

Nights, I would lie awake in that cold, black room of strangers all sleeping together, some of them mumbling in their sleep or crying out or snoring, chamber pots under the beds and bad smells in the air, my hand under the pillow clutching Pa's shot bag, and I'd wonder if I'd ever see home again.

Night after night, I'd put myself to sleep remembering the happiest time of my life when I shot my first rabbit and thought I was dead from the terrible kick of the gun, and I opened my eyes and there was John looking so worried. And then we all ate rabbit stew.

When I couldn't stand the loneliness anymore, one evening just before supper, I went down to see Mrs. Eddington and I asked her about going home. "My dear," she said, "your mother cannot keep you. You are here to stay."

"But Ma said it would only be for a short time," I protested.

She stroked my hair gently. "Perhaps you misunderstood. Or your mother could not bear to tell you . . ."

I began to weep.

"There, there," she said.

That only increased my sorrow. I wanted more than anything to be *there, there*.

But I was stuck *here, here*.

Forever and ever?

I would end up like Sally, who didn't know any other home besides this and would probably never know any other place. It was too terrible to believe: to be locked up indoors away from the wind and the sun and growing things forever. How could Ma do this, send me away and forget me?

I was going up the stairs slowly after this dreadful conversation with Mrs. Eddington when — wouldn't you know it — Emmeline Sue was heading directly down toward me.

Moses-Poses
Moses-Poses
No one knows
Where she gets her clo —

I didn't let her finish. I cut off the last word. I was smaller than she was, but faster. I used my shoulder to bump into her hip hard, and then when she tilted to one side, I grabbed her hands and held them tight behind her.

"I'll shoot you dead," I whispered quick in her ear. "I got my Pa's gun. I carried it here from the prairie. I carry it wherever I go. You better be careful or I'll shoot you dead. I swear it."

She was squirming and struggling so hard I couldn't hold her hands anymore. I let her go.

"Big talk." She stuck out her tongue. "I don't believe you." But she backed off a little.

"Be on the lookout for me," I said, "tonight. After lights out."

I walked on.

Once I was in my bed, I lay still till all around me girls were sleeping. I reached for Pa's shot bag and took out one of his bullets.

Emmeline Sue was tossing about under her covers this way and that as if her thoughts had turned into ants that were crawling all over her and biting her.

Twice, she sat up quick and looked around, then slowly lay back down. No one's more scared than a scared bully.

I waited, leaving plenty of time for her to get lots of those worry bites.

After I figured she had fretted enough, I got out of bed and tiptoed 'round to where the big lump of her head was on her pillow. "Here's proof," I whispered, pressing the cold metal bullet down on her forehead right between her eyes — exactly where I had got my rabbit. "This is where I aim for. You just better watch yourself."

Her hand slowly reached up and her fingers clasped around that smooth lead pellet resting there.

I took a step back.

I heard a gasp.

Turning around, I tiptoed back to my bed.

Clutching the soft leather shot bag close to my heart, I closed my eyes, and my last thought was a happy one:

I am Annie, the girl with a gun.

6

EMMELINE SUE SMATHERS, the bully, was scared.

So scared that my life would be a little easier for a while. But for how long?

Bullies don't stay peaceable long or they wouldn't be bullies.

Then what?

My gun — Pa's gun — was far away, and even if I'd had it there in the infirmary, so what? I could never shoot a person!

I would remain Moses-Poses till I died. The county farm was my home now forever.

I was doomed.

Or so I thought . . .

The very next day, destiny took a hand.

A shiny new buggy pulled by a fine black horse drove up to the county farm and parked, and a nicely dressed man came in to see Mrs. Eddington. He wore a jacket and a tie, and his black hair was slicked down flat. He was a farmer who lived some miles away. He had come because he and his wife had a new baby boy and they needed a girl to help care for the child.

I guess my name came first to Mrs. Eddington's

mind because of our recent unhappy conversation. She
sent for me at once.

"Would you like to work for this gentleman and his
family? They will pay you fifty cents a week, which
they'll send to your mother, and they will see that you
go to school. In return, you will care for their new
baby. Think it over, Annie."

I didn't have to think it over. To be out of there? To
be free? To get schoolin' and to be on a farm and
outdoors again?

"Yes," I said at once, eagerly. "Oh yes. I'm good
with babies. I took care of my two baby sisters, Hulda
and Emily."

He was going to give me a nice home and pay me —
and send me to school! It was almost more than I could
believe.

"If she's a-willin', I'm a-willin'," the farmer said.
"She looks right healthy. She can just collect her duds
and come along with me now."

"Oh, no," Mrs. Eddington said. "I need her mother's permission."

He looked disappointed. "I was countin' on takin'
her home today. The missus could use help."

"I must write to her mother." Mrs. Eddington was
firm.

"Can you do it right quick?" The farmer was so
anxious, it seemed like these folks really wanted me
bad.

I held my breath, scared of what he might say next.

He could've said, "Gimme someone else. Gimme an orphan who can just come along with me now." But he didn't.

"I'll write today," she reassured him. "I am always so pleased when I can place one of my charges — in a good *Christian* home?" It was kind of a question.

"Every single Sunday," he boasted. "We're church-goin' folk." He was grumpy, but her promise seemed to satisfy him.

As for me, I could hardly wait. This family was really *looking forward* to having *me* with them!

"I'm glad for you, Annie," Sally said, when I told her. Her lips trembled, and she turned her face away so I couldn't see. "Real glad."

That night I heard her crying in her bed.

"I'm sorry to leave you," I whispered to her, "but I need to go, Sally. *I can't live here.*"

"I know," she said, weeping.

"I got to go before Emmeline starts up on her 'Moses-Poses' again. I got to."

"I understand, Annie. Really I do. I'm prayin' for you."

Ma sent back a letter with her approval. Mrs. Eddington helped me get ready, and while we were putting my things together, I got a wonderful, dangerous idea.

Out of nowhere — suddenly — it flew into my head

and made me shiver because it was so risky. It meant
breaking my word and giving away a secret that wasn't
really mine, but I decided to chance it.

"Mrs. Eddington." I tried to control my shaky voice.
"I need to tell you a secret. Sally knows how to sew as
nice as me. And she can already read and write real
good. She has her own copybook that's neater'n mine,
and she's very smart. Do you think she —" I stopped,
scared, but then I finished all in a rush "— could be
your helper and go to school in my place?"

"Sally?" Both Mrs. Eddington's voice and her eyebrows went flying up in surprise. "Sally Jones? But
the child barely says a word. The other children call
her Silent Sally."

"She can talk more'n you think," I said, "but private. You see, she's scared of all the bullies and how
they'd make fun of her. That's why she's silent. Private, she's really very smart."

"How do *you* know all this?"

"We study together, Ma'am. In the old storeroom."

"Hmmm." Mrs. Eddington rubbed her chin with
her fingertips. "She does sew nicely. Silent Sally? She
reads and writes? Are you sure now?"

"Yes, Ma'am. It's her special secret —"

"Don't worry, child. It's safe with me. I will certainly look into it," she promised. "Sally would be a
very convenient helper for me because she already lives
here and is familiar with the routine. Thank you, Annie. You're quite a girl."

Mrs. Eddington looked at me with the strangest expression on her face, as if I'd sprouted donkey ears or angel wings or something uncommon.

I just barely had time to say goodbye to Sally. "Speak up when the time comes for Mrs. Eddington to interview you," I urged. "Talking might get you a chance to go to school."

"I'll talk plenty," Sally promised. "I'll run her ears off. And I'll never forget you, Annie."

"Me either," I said. "And I'll speak to you at night in the darkness, wherever I am. Even if you can't hear me, you'll know."

Sally had a generous heart. She was truly glad for me. "You're so lucky to go away to live with a nice family."

We hugged and hugged.

"I can't bear to be right beside you and let you go. I want to grab you and hold on to my friend-sister." Her voice broke. "I'm going upstairs to stand at the window and watch —"

She choked off her words and scooted away, leaving me — sitting carefully, trying not to wrinkle my good dress — waiting in the office until the farmer arrived.

We drove down the driveway away from the poorhouse, me waving back wildly at Sally, who leaned out the window so far I feared she'd fall.

I smiled to myself. I smiled so big, I thought my face would crack, and I ducked my head down to the side so the farmer wouldn't see. As the buggy approached their farm, my mind told the ending over and over like one of the fairy stories of Pa's: *And so Annie lived happily ever after!*

I will never write down the name of that farmer and his wife.

I will never say their names out loud. I gave them their fitting names — *the wolves!*

Mr. wolf and Mrs. wolf.

I came to their home with such high hopes and dreams.

During that buggy ride I was already talking to Sally in my mind. "I will work hard and love their baby and learn to read and write and spell till I can write my own letters home to Ma, and I can read hers back to me. Once I can read and write, Sal, I'll write to you, too."

And I carried along Sally's happiness for me. "You're so lucky, Annie."

When we got to the farm, the hard-faced wife, who had a chin like the letter *V* and big, sharp, white upper teeth that poked out, was waiting in the messy kitchen to tell me the household routine.

I will set it down here just as she said it.

"The baby is most important. He must be cared for whenever he needs it. Mind, I am a very tenderhearted mother. I don't want to hear my baby crying or ever see a sore, red bottom. Ever! I couldn't bear that!

"You'll have a few other duties around here, of

course. You must be up at four in the morning to prepare breakfast. Biscuits, fried cornmeal mush, bacon, potatoes, and coffee is what we eat.

"Then you will go to the barn and milk the cows," she continued. "That is part of your job. Carry the milk to the kitchen and skim it, and carry it out to the little wooden house over the spring to stay cool.

"Feed the pigs and calves. That is another part of your job.

"The dishes and pots must be carefully washed.

"Laundry is, of course, part of your job. And sewing." She stared at me hard. "You do *know* how to sew, girl?"

"Yes, Ma'am."

"You will pick the vegetables for meals from the garden.

"Midday dinner — the big meal — is your responsibility, as well as supper.

"You'll eat after we're through, from what's left over. I will dish the food out on your plate to make sure that you get your just portion."

She showed me where to leave my things behind a rough wood screen in a shadowed corner of the kitchen, near the trundle bed where I would sleep. "The baby will sleep right by you, of course, so you can hear him if he frets.

"Time to get out of your good dress now, girl. There's lots of work to be done. You've been a great inconvenience. We expected you more'n a week ago."

My supper was bread heels and some gravy the

farmer's wife spooned out onto a dented tin plate. "It's rich meat gravy," she said. "Better'n you're used to in the poorhouse, I'm sure."

Late late that night, ever so late, after supper dishes were washed and the baby was finally asleep, I crept into my lumpy trundle bed and closed my eyes and spoke to Sally.

"I am not lucky, Sally," I said into the darkness. "This man and his wife are cruel. They do not like me. I do not think I will fare well here."

In the darkness, I could imagine Sally's bright kind face, and it comforted me.

That image of my friend and my memories of my family were all the comfort I had for the next year or so. I lost track of time in my numbing weariness.

Nights, my mind jumped back to Pa, so long ago, sitting in front of the fire in the evenings, talking about the war between the North and the South. Pa hated slavery. He believed it was unjust for one person to own another. "People are not property," he would always finish sadly. "No matter what their color, they have their rights."

Now Pa was long dead and that Civil War he hated was past, and all those black slaves were free.

But I was a different kind of slave here.

The wolves owned me. That's what slavery is all about: every minute of my day or night belonged to them and they could hit me and punish me as they liked.

I was nine years old.

I had no rights.

To live that way is terrible.

I had been too young to understand Pa's talk — till now.

How glad I was that the Union had won and the slaves were free.

Glory, hallelujah!

7

MRS. WOLF WAS A SHREW. She could be laughing with her husband one minute and then screaming at me the next. When screaming didn't suffice, she'd hit me — on the side of my face, on my back, wherever she could reach.

Mr. wolf hit, too, but not so often. Mostly he said nasty things about how stupid I was and what did he expect from poorhouse trash?

When I'd been there several months, one evening I tripped in my tiredness on the way to the springhouse and I spilled some milk. Not a great deal, maybe a half cupful, but he happened to come along just then and see me. I had set the pails down to rest myself.

He was wearing wading boots, and he came up to me and kicked me in my leg so hard, I could barely stand. "Lummox!" he bellowed. "You water the ground with my milk!"

I picked up the pails and, barely able to move, struggled on my way.

Later that evening, he demanded, "Why are you limpin'? I am not payin' good wages for a cripple. I told Mrs. Eddington I wanted a healthy girl. If you're lame, right back you go."

Wonderful, I thought. *Suits me. I'll just limp harder and you'll have to take me back. Living there with Emmeline Sue and the others would be much better than living here with you.*

So I limped about my tasks for months afterward, even after the bruises and the pain were gone. But the farmer and his wife didn't take me back. They only mocked me.

I learned to be more silent than Sally.

"I have a letter from your mother," Mrs. wolf said one day. My heart quickened when I recognized that beloved, familiar handwriting, tiny and neat. I reached for it.

"You can't read," she scorned. "I'll read it for you." Her eye barely glanced at the paper. "Your family is well and glad to have your wages," she said, carelessly putting the paper down smack in a puddle of pork grease on the kitchen table.

I tried to save it, but she grabbed it back quickly and began ripping it into small pieces and dropping the shreds into the kindling box. "We can't pile up need-less junk," she said. "I'll write to your mother and tell her how very happy you are here. She'll be glad to hear it."

Weeks and more weeks crept by. One afternoon, when she was in a good mood, I asked her, "Please, Ma'am, am I to have books and go to school?"

She laughed harshly and didn't say anything, but I heard her repeating my question to the he-wolf. He did bring me an old speller.

"You can go to school three mornings," he said, "if you get all your chores done."

I did go a few times, but he'd let them know at the school that I was an infirmary girl and the children mocked me and splashed mud on me.

When I studied the speller at home, while I was rocking the baby, Mrs. wolf was furious. "Pay attention to what you're doing," she screamed. "You'll drop my precious baby." When I propped the book up near the dishpan, she complained, "Those dishes need to be washed clean. Close the book!"

So I gave it up.

The baby was a good little boy, but his small slitty eyes made him ugly-looking. I could hardly like him because I knew how he'd grow up.

It wasn't his fault, but he was a little wolf.

I took good care of him, but I never loved him the way I'd loved Emily and Hulda. *Poor little wolf cub*, I'd think, rocking him. *One day you'll grow up to be a big wolf.*

In fact, I noticed that his ears were already slightly pointy. I began to gently stretch the upper tips of his ears a little and massage them, so they'd grow pointier and folks would recognize right off he was a wolf.

We went on that way for a very long time, them in their meanness and me in my misery. They *were* church-going folks — every Sunday morning regular — but it didn't seem to affect them. They never carried a thing home from God's house.

Except the one Sunday they took the baby along in

a blue sailor suit and a white hat with a blue ribbon on it to show him off.

He carried something home all right.

Mumps!

I took real good care of him. He had a mild case, a couple of bad days of fever and then he began to recover.

Next, Mr. wolf came down with it, and he gave it to Mrs. wolf. The two of them looked more than passing strange all swollen up like pumpkins. They both had terrible cases, first high fevers, then chills, with sore throats and earaches and fierce, blinding headaches.

"How come we got it and the poorhouse brat didn't get it?" I overheard him grumble.

"Be glad she can do the chores." The she-wolf was impatient with him.

And then he asked me, "How come you didn't catch this sickness?"

"I'm lucky, I guess," I said.

I wouldn't tell him I'd already had it.

He inspected me daily, waiting, hoping I'd catch it. He really hated that I stayed healthy.

I did have to work harder while they were sick, but it was worth it. I was so glad! Nights, I would lie in the trundle bed and bury my head under the pillow and laugh and laugh.

God knew just what He was doing when He sent mumps home with them from church.

From then on, every Sunday afternoon I'd watch

hopefully to see if anything else came home with them from church.

Measles? Scarlet fever? Chicken pox?

Too bad. Nothing else came.

My tenth birthday passed, but I didn't hardly notice.

One night late, I was sitting by the fireside darning a sock, and I was so weary, I fell sound asleep. How do I know? Because Mrs. wolf crept up to me and slapped me so hard on the side of my head, she knocked the darning egg with the sock clear into the fire.

"You lazy good-for-nothing. How dare you sleep when you're working?" she screamed. "Now look what you've done."

Inside my head, I said, *Serves you right.* As I watched the fire burn, I silently told Sally, *Not me, Sal. I didn't do it. Mrs. wolf burned the sock and charred the darning egg.* She *did it and she knows it, too.*

I could not stay there anymore, or I would turn into a wolf, as well.

That night I began to lay my plans. "I'm going to run away, Sally," I resolved. "As soon as I can. I'm going to run as far away from the wolves as possible."

I needed the exact proper time to go, so that they wouldn't catch me and haul me back. Every day, I did my endless chores; I cooked and I washed up and I rocked the baby and I milked the cows and I carried the milk carefully without spilling a drop and I fed the pigs. Wash days, I did the laundry and ironed.

Every night when I was, at last, lying still in the kitchen shadows, I would report to Sally. "Not yet, but soon. I know the time is coming."

Weeks and more weeks passed. I noted the way Mr. wolf headed when he drove to town for provisions. I asked a peddler selling cloth if town was walking distance, and he said he reckoned so for any good pair of feet.

I had me a good pair of feet. I would walk there to catch the train. I had no money for fare, but I would figure something out. I had to!

Then, like a new spring flower suddenly pushing up and blooming through a crack in winter's cold hard ground, my chance appeared.

Mr. and Mrs. wolf decided to take the baby and go on a day trip to visit kin over Indiana way. First she recited a long list of instructions for me. After she wound up, she warned, "Mind! Idle hands are the devil's workshop."

"Yes'm," I said.

They drove off holidaying.

Run, Annie run! was my first thought as I watched the buggy's dust settle on the road. *Run fast!*

No, Mrs. Eddington sent me here, and if I don't leave things right she will hear about it and be blamed.

Besides, everyone knows how sneaky wolves are.

Who's to say they wouldn't turn around and come back after the first half hour just to see what I was about?

Hard as it was, I didn't run away at once. But no one ever did chores faster. I washed up the breakfast wares, and then I milked those cows so quick they mooed in protest.

"Sorry," I said, patting each one on the flank gently as I moved on. "Poor things, you got to stay here, but I got to go — fast."

Not the pigs. They were happy that the slops came so fast. I squealed them a loud goodbye. *"Ooeeink!"*

Like a tornado, I whirled through that house, sweeping and dusting. I ironed his church shirt and her petticoats — but I didn't do the ruffles; she didn't deserve nice ruffles — and I folded and put away the laundry.

That last day, as I worked, I sang along, a song my dear dead sister Mary Jane used to sing as she worked about our house.

> 'Mid pleasures and palaces though we may
> roam,
> Be it ever so humble, there's no place like
> home . . .

This was the single time I ever sang in that wretched farmhouse.

By the time all my work was done, the sun was high. I had to get far away as fast as possible.

I had one final problem. I didn't know how to write well enough to leave a note, but I needed them to understand they were un-Christian and vicious and I hated them.

What to do? Someone else might have given up and just gone, but not me.

I had that stubbornness in me that Ma worried about.

While I was gathering up my few belongings to put into a little bundle, I found myself talking aloud to Sally. "They're grown-up bullies. That's worse than Emmeline Sue, much worse, 'cause 'grown-up' means they oughta know better, right, Sal?"

And that gave me the clue.

I went and got Pa's shot bag. Excitedly, I took out one of his bullets. I set it in a dry bread heel right on the dented tin plate they'd made me eat on, and I poured old cold gravy on it and placed that plate with my supper and the bullet in it right at the head of their table.

I hoped they were smart enough to figure out my message:

THIS IS WHAT YOU DESERVE!

8

Goodbye wolves, my heart sang. *I know you'll howl when you find me gone. I'm so glad I won't be able to hear you.*

First, I skipped down the three porch steps, then I hopped along the pebbled path that led away from that hated farmhouse. Next, without a single look back, I turned onto the main road and started heading toward town.

For hours and hours, I walked steadily, stopping only when I heard wagon wheels or voices. Each time, I ducked down real deep in the brush and hid as low as I could get. I didn't want any of the local folks to be able to tell them, "She headed this-a-ways" or "that-a-ways."

Just being out in the fresh air and seeing the fields and the open road winding far ahead thrilled me. I whistled greetings to the birds that flew above. I called out "Hello!" first to a rabbit that hopped past and then to every living critter I saw. Hello hello hello hello. I was greeting the whole world!

Only one small question kept running through my mind to mar my journey: *How will I pay for a train ticket?* I kept pushing that question away. Without a penny in my pocket, how could I answer it?

When I came to a stream running near the road, I stopped and waded, cooling my tired feet. I washed the sweat off my face and neck, and I wet down the top of my head and my plait so my hair'd be neat.

Spying some blackberry bushes nearby, I whooped with joy and began to eat my fill. Pa would've smiled. "This time I *almost* ate more'n I picked," I told his memory.

Every few minutes I'd peek back over my shoulder to see if any two-legged vicious critter was prowling behind.

In all the time since I'd left the poorhouse — more than one full year — never once had I had the chance to roam outdoors, to run and skip and play. Truly, I had been their prisoner and slave.

And now I was free, free, *free!* I would get to the railroad station somehow and I would get on that train to Greenville. From there I could surely find my way back to Ma and my sisters and John. Find my way home. *Home!*

Tired as my feet were, once I saw way up ahead the rooftops of the town with the railway station, I told them, "Feet, you got to hurry."

My feet obeyed. They speeded up.

They began to run till I could hardly breathe.

That didn't matter a whit. I felt so light, I was practically flying!

"Thank you, feet," I said, remembering my manners. "Thank you for your quick steppin'."

And then I was there at last, standing near the tracks of the station for the Dayton & Union Railroad.

I peeked back over my shoulder, then all around one last time. No one was following me. Hurrah!

A truly remarkable-looking couple was waiting there already, next to a whopping stack of metal-banded wooden trunks and leather bags and boxes.

He was a tall, fierce-looking gentleman in a stovepipe hat, and in his hand he carried a big black rolled umbrella with a silver handle that flashed in the bright sunlight. This was odd, because there wasn't a cloud in the sky. His long, thin face was decorated with lovely black side-whiskers.

Beside him stood a short round lady with a button nose on which sat spectacles. Both of them were beautifully, expensively dressed in black, head to toe. Mrs. Eddington had taught me about fabrics, and I could see they were wearing the best, she fine taffeta and he woolens.

"Please, Ma'am," I began. I was breathing hard. "Is this where — I get the train — for Greenville?"

"With the Lord's help, any time now," she said. "We're waiting for that very train." Looking over her spectacles, she studied me front and sideways. "You've been running, young lady. You know it's unseemly for ladies to run."

"Yes, Ma'am."

"Mmm. What's your name, dear?" Her voice was gentle and sweet as molasses, but her face was no-nonsense stern.

"Annie Moses."

"This is my husband, the Reverend Sylvester Bunbury, and I am his wife, Honoria Bunbury." Now she smiled at me.

Two splendid names. I had never met such grand folks before. I bowed my head politely. "Ma'am. Sir."

"*Siste, viator*—" the reverend said sharply, and he pointed the umbrella directly at me.

I looked to the lady for help.

"That means, 'Pause, traveler,' " she explained softly. "The Reverend Sylvester loves languages and is particularly partial to Latin. We are going abroad, so he may continue his language studies in Germany. He will teach Latin as he learns German. I translate for him, child."

I was awed by all this.

Then he spoke again. "I trust you are not absquatulating from your kin. You're not absconding, are you?"

Dazzled as I was by these gorgeous words, I did not understand them, so I couldn't answer.

She turned to him. "Sylvester, dear, she does not look to me like a girl who would run away from her family."

"Well—" I began.

I didn't know what to say. To make it this far and

then get sent back would be awful. He was staring at me with his sharp gray eyes, while his wife again inspected me *above* her spectacles, as though they were a fence to be looked over and not through.

I did a terrible thing then. Ma would have been ashamed of me.

I didn't quite lie, yet I didn't tell the truth.

I half lied. "No," I said. "I am not running away from my family."

"Well, you appear to me to be exceedingly juvenescent to be peregrinating on your own initiative," the Reverend Sylvester observed. "You'd best remain here, beside Honoria. She'll shelter you."

Mrs. Honoria tucked me right between herself and the pile of baggage. I felt terrible. These people were being so nice to me, and I had just half lied to them, and soon they would find out I had no money for a ticket! What would they think of me then?

I stood there, wondering about what I could do or say to straighten things out, but nothing came into my mind. I was in the worst pickle of my life.

Just then the train came, driving everything out of my mind. I was mighty glad I was standing with them right then because the noise was earsplitting and scary. First, there was this loud, loud steam whistle, and after it a bell on the locomotive began to clang.

The train stopped, giving off steam in huge puffs, and the brakes squealed long like a passel of pigs at slaughter. I guess I looked scared for a lot of reasons.

Mrs. Honoria patted my shoulder. "Your first train trip?" she inquired.

I nodded.

Well, it took ever so much lifting and hauling and squeezing to get all their luggage on board but, at last, we got on that train, too, and sat down in big comfortable seats.

I had one all to myself and was glad of it. Escaping from the wolves had left me tuckered out.

The engine blasted another fierce noise like a million scissor grindstones whirling and sparking all at once. Then the brakes squealed again and we started off.

"Tell us, Annie," Mrs. Honoria asked, "how come you to be traveling alone?"

I looked at her kind face, and I burst right into tears. "I lied outside," I confessed. "I am wicked. I knew lying was wrong, but I couldn't help it. I'm so sorry. Please forgive me. I *am* running away!"

"Oh dear." Mrs. Honoria was most distressed. "And we helped you —" Flustered, she looked to her husband.

"We aided and abetted," the Reverend Sylvester said slowly, thumping the umbrella hard on the floor at every second word. "Did your family abuse you? Were they cruel? Or was the problem *res angusta domi?*"

" '*Not enough money at home?*' " whispered Mrs. Honoria.

"It's not my folks I'm running from. My folks live in

North Star. That's a-ways from here, in Darke County. I'm running away from — um — slaveholders?" I struggled to explain. It was mighty hard to make a man who spoke Latin understand plain English. "See — it's my folks I'm running *to* —" I began to blubber so much I couldn't talk.

"Now, now," Mrs. Honoria said. She drew me to her and held me close as I cried. No mother had comforted me for almost two years. I wept so long. I guess the Bunburys grew alarmed at the thought that they'd soon get soaked.

"Sylvester," she said, "have you a handkerchief for Annie?"

He pulled out a napkin almost the size of a pillowcase and gave it to me, and I stopped crying and blew my nose and apologized a dozen times.

"Shh . . ." Mrs. Honoria fished around in her huge black purse and came up with a lemon drop dipped in sugar.

"For you, child."

"Now elucidate, Annie," the Reverend Sylvester said. "Clarify." And when he saw I still didn't understand, he added, "Explicate."

"Tell us about it," Mrs. Honoria said helpfully.

So I told them all about the wolves. I told them everything. I showed them the bruises on my neck near my ear and on my arms and my legs.

As I talked, they both made sympathetic noises with their tongues — *tsk tsk* — though they weren't sucking lemon drops.

When I was all finished, the Reverend Sylvester said hotly, "You did nothing wicked, child. Those were not good Christians. I'm gratified we facilitated your journey. *Satis verborum.*"

" '*Enough of words,*' " Mrs. Honoria translated.

"I'm in worse trouble. I don't have a train ticket," I admitted.

"No matter," the Reverend Sylvester thumped again, hard. "Mrs. Bunbury and I will enthusiastically underwrite your passage. My spouse and I have long been abolitionists —"

She came to my rescue, seeing I had trouble understanding her kind husband. His beautiful big words were like stars on those very bright nights when the whole sky is lit up so that it's impossible to separate them out and recognize each one.

"Let me explain to the child, dear." She addressed me. "Sylvester and I have always been against involuntary servitude. That is, slavery." As she spoke, her face became pink with anger. Her bosom heaved and rustled. "You did the right thing to run away. Sylvester?" She looked at him.

"Well put, Honoria. Estimably pronounced." He coughed and harumphed. "Like another child of God named Moses long ago in Egypt, you fled from bondage."

"Amen!" Mrs. Honoria said heartily. "A-*men!*"

I loved the two of them from that moment on.

9

I SAT THERE happily riding alongside them, while the train clacked and rocked and the whistle hooted through the villages and the prairie.

After a while, Mrs. Honoria fetched down a neat wicker picnic hamper from the shelf overhead. "Teatime," she said, "only we've lemonade instead. It travels better. You must join us, Annie."

"No thank you, Ma'am,"

Three times she offered and three times I refused. Refusing was the hardest thing I ever did — I was a-feared my stomach would rumble out *yes* and give the lie to my words — but Ma had taught me manners. I had to be polite.

"You *will* join us in a collation, Annie," the Reverend Sylvester said, with a thump of his umbrella that settled things.

Mrs. Honoria unpacked several lovely linen napkins, each with a large curlicued *B* embroidered in black in one corner, and from other such linens she brought forth what looked like a million small sandwiches. She handed me the very first one, explaining, "The Reverend Sylvester is partial to cucumber."

And that's what they all were — cucumber!

I'd never seen such lovely sandwiches. Soft, dainty rounds of buttered white bread without crusts, stuffed to bursting with paper-thin sliced cucumber, each slice with fluted edges, nicely flavored in brine.

"How do you bake bread without a crust, Mrs. Honoria?" I wondered.

"Bless me, child, you don't. You trim the loaf."

"Then what do you do with the crust?"

Since Mrs. Honoria's mouth was full, the reverend answered. "Feed it to the *avis*." Then he translated for himself, "The birds." He happily bit into a sandwich.

My face must have shown my shock at such wastefulness.

"Now, Sylvester" — Mrs. Honoria put three more sandwiches on the napkin in my lap — "you mustn't tease. You know we use the crusts in bread pudding."

I think I ate a dozen sandwiches, at least. I meant to keep track, but I lost count watching the reverend. He ate seventeen. I did have two cups of lemonade; it was delicious — sweet, not tart. I was so glad it wasn't tea.

When the conductor came through, the Reverend Sylvester took out money for my ticket and handed it over. "We didn't know until the last minute that Cousin —" He paused for a second.

The conductor had dug out a handful of coins and was carefully counting the change.

"— Cousin Annie *Oakley* — this lovely young lady" — he pointed at me — "was journeying with us." He winked at me. "She's my wife's kin. The Oakleys are real pioneer stock, eh, Annie?"

"Yes, Cousin Sylvester," I said. "We've been farmin' hereabouts since Grandpa and Grandma came out from Pennsylvania in a Conestoga wagon."

The conductor nodded agreeably as he punched my ticket, and he went on his way.

"You caught on very well," Mrs. Honoria said once he was gone. "Sylvester was covering your tracks there, dear. He thinks of everything."

"I am beholden to you," I said. "One day I will pay you back."

"Don't fret about it, child. Accept it as a gift now, and then forget it," Mrs. Honoria advised. "By the way, my family name is Smith, not Oakley."

I was bewildered. "Then where'd the *Oakley* come from?" I asked the reverend.

"I was born and raised in a sweet little town named Oakley," he said. "I've always had a fondness for the name. It has a nice, solid ring to it." His smile was wicked. "No one will be able to trace you, child, *Dei gratia.*"

" *'God willing!'* " Mrs. Honoria murmured.

"Mrs. Honoria?" I asked. "Do you speak Latin, too?"

"No, child, I only translate."

She dusted crumbs from her lap with a napkin and then helped me brush myself off.

Her answer didn't exactly make sense to me, but I had no time to inquire further because just then the train was beginning to slow down.

By this time it was dusk, getting on toward night.

"Greenville!" the conductor began to shout. "Greenville! Next stop, Greenville!"

Suddenly I was a little scared about being left off alone in a strange place at night. My knees began to tremble.

Like magic, it seemed, Mrs. Honoria read my mind. "I shall get off briefly with you, Annie, and put you in someone's care," she said. "Sylvester will see that the train does not depart for Cincinnati without me."

I went over and hugged the Reverend Sylvester, who was real wet around his eyes. "The coal dust —" he said, and he harumphed a whole bunch.

"Thank you," I said. "Thank you so much."

"It was nothing, child. Nothing. *Pax vobiscum.*"

" *'Peace be with you,'* " Mrs. Honoria said, as she grasped my hand firmly and hustled me off the train and into the Greenville station ticket office. "This child has to get to North Star Village," she said to the young man there. "Do you know of anyone going that route who might carry her along?"

"North Star? Well . . ." He tapped his cheek and looked mighty serious. Then he smiled. "Yep. Matter of fact, you're in luck. The mail carrier, Joseph Shaw, is runnin' late today. He goes up that route, and he's just now out back loadin' up parcels from the luggage room. She can ride along with him."

The train whistled a warning.

"Much obliged," Mrs. Honoria said, and she and I hurried out the door and round the back.

There we saw a saggy-back horse and a worn wagon

parked. An elderly, bald man with a kind face — gray beard but no side-whiskers growing — was piling boxes in back.

The train whistled again. "You'd best go, Mrs. Honoria," I said.

"Don't fret, child. The reverend will confound the conductor with his Latin, and they'll hold the train."

"They won't understand his Latin without you." I was anxious.

"That's how he'll confound 'em." She smiled mischievously. Then she went up to old Mr. Shaw and told him where I was bound.

"I'd be glad a' the company," he said.

"Then I'll leave Annie here with you." Quickly, Mrs. Honoria put three more sugared lemon drops in my hand. "Eat one now and keep the others for the way," she advised.

The train whistle warned for the third time.

"Goodbye, Annie." She kissed me right on the top of my head. "God keep you safe."

"I'll never forget you, Mrs. Honoria."

"Nor we you," she promised. She started away, turned back once to blow a kiss, and was gone.

When old Mr. Shaw had arranged all the parcels in the wagon to his liking, we set out at last, me beside him on the wagon seat, silent. The road was pitted with holes and ruts so it was hard driving, and I guessed he wasn't much of a talker.

I was so full of the extraordinary events of the day, I just sat dumb beside him, and we rode that way for an hour or more before I offered him a lemon drop, which he took.

"Mighty tasty," he said, after a bit. "Thank 'ee."

"Mrs. Honoria — that lady who left me — she gave them to me. Her husband is a reverend. He talks Latin. They're on their way to Germany so he can learn German, too."

"Mmm. Fancy that! Grand folks." Mr. Shaw was rightly impressed. We rode quiet awhile more.

"Who are the kin in North Star you're a-goin' to, Annie?"

"My ma. Her name is Susan Brumbaugh — that was Susan Moses."

Mr. Joseph Shaw almost fell out of his very own wagon. "Whoa! Whoa!" He reined up the horse and stopped right there in the middle of the road. "Here now, girl. What're you tellin' me? What's *your* name?"

"Annie."

"Susan Brumbaugh don't have no Annie."

"She does, too. I'm her!"

"Wait a minute." He took out a handkerchief and mopped his shiny head. "You must be Phoebe Anne . . ." He looked at me hard.

"Yes," I admitted. "That is, I was Phoebe Anne Moses, but I hate that name."

"I never would've thought it," he said, astonished. "I plumb never would've figured this one. Well,

Phoebe Anne — or Annie — I got news for you. I'm your new pa. Your ma and me is married."

It was my turn to almost fall out of the wagon.

"True?"

"Nothing could be truer in the world." He chuckled. "Oh, Susan will be mighty pleased to see what I brought back with the mail today. Mighty, mighty pleased."

He was so delighted, he drove along talking to himself for a good while. "Well, fancy that!" he said a half dozen times. "Can you beat that!" And he hammered his thigh hard with his fist at the pleasure of it.

He gave me the news of my family, which I was hungry for. My three older sisters, Lydia, Elizabeth, and Sarah Ellen, were married and gone away. Ma and the younger children lived on his farm in the new cabin he'd built — two stories with two rooms up and two downstairs.

Why hadn't Ma sent for me, I wondered, *if things were good?*

Ma was still doing nursing for the district.

That was why. It meant money was still short.

"You can jes' call me Grandpap," he said. "That's what your brother and sisters call me, and I like it. It makes me feel close to y'all. One family —"

Now that we were kin, he felt free to tell me his troubles. He confided that times were very hard at home. He had owned a farm and sold it, intending to buy another, but a swindler had done him out of all the money except for five hundred dollars.

"I put that five hundred dollars as down payment on this farm," he said sadly, "but the mortgage is so big that the interest I got to pay is ruinin' us. Ruinin' us." He shook his head.

"I'll try to help, Grandpap." I promised. "Truly I will."

He was pleased by my words, but he didn't credit them. "How can a slip of a girl help? You mean well, child, but I think there's no help."

"You'll see," I promised. "You just wait."

"There's North Star comin' up yonder," he said, pointing.

"I'm going to duck under this old lap rug and hide," I told him, "while you go in and tell Johnny and Hulda and Emily to come out and carry in the bundles."

I squeezed down low and covered myself, and he tucked me in real good all around so nothing of me was showing — and right straight up to the cabin we drove. Well . . .

In a minute, Johnny and Hulda and Emily came a running out. They lifted that old raggedy rug, and I jumped up at once, shouting, "Surprise! Annie ho! Annie ho! Annie ho!"

Johnny began to laugh and laugh and Hulda tried to climb up into the wagon and baby Emily started to holler real loud because I was just a stranger to her. I picked her up and held her to stop her bawling. "It's me," I said. "It's Annie. Your big sister. You remember me." I tickled her with kisses. In a minute, she was snuggling up and hugging me real tight.

Then out came Ma carrying the soup ladle Pa had carved for her, eager to see what all the ruckus was about. She looked around and when she saw me, she dropped that ladle (it didn't break — Pa carved true) and Ma held out her arms and Baby Emily and I were out of the wagon in no time and into them.

I was *home*!

10

Home!

Those two years of lonely nights, the first lying awake in the poorhouse ward and the second tossing and turning in the trundle bed in my enemies' shadowy farm kitchen, were over!

Here was John chattering away about learning to shoot at last, his brown eyes sparking joy; and Emily and Hulda climbing all over me, both trying to sit on my lap, while all four of us grinned and giggled and poked each other, first out of shyness, then out of silliness, and altogether out of love.

I was bursting to tell about Emmeline Sue, and the mean farmer and his wife and their homely baby with the pointed ears who brought mumps home from church.

I would've told, but looking at my happy brother and sisters, I knew they were too young to hear about the evil creatures who lurked outside North Star, people who were more like the monsters in the spooky tales Pa used to tell so long ago.

Ugly. Greedy. Cruel. Dishonest.

I didn't have many nice things to relate. I did describe Sally Jones and her jackstones, and the Bunburys, and what a terrible-wonderful experience it is to ride on a train. And I told all about the picnic lunch: the linen napkins and lemonade and cucumber sandwiches without crusts!

And Latin.

"Can you say some Latin words?" John begged.

I shook my head.

"What does it sound like?"

"*Ibbada bibbida baabade boo.* Something like that. Only grander."

Then I actually remembered one Latin word, the one that the Reverend Sylvester had translated for himself. "Wait —" I said. "*Avis* is Latin for 'birds.' "

Everybody took a turn saying it, as if they were tasting Latin. It sounded so strange. John particularly liked the sounds. "*Av-is.*" He licked his lips afterward.

Ma stood over us, smiling. "Latin is a very old language. Thousands of years old. Only very educated people know Latin."

Then it was time for her to shoo the younger children off to bed. Grandpap Shaw, weary from our journey, retired, too, saying at least three times before we went, "That was the best load of mail I ever picked up in Greenville."

"Thee must be hungry," Ma said. "Wash and sit down."

I sat me down to thick hot soup full of carrots and turnips and green beans and potatoes. On the table stood a basket of crusty fresh bread and butter — this supper I was going to eat as many slices as I wanted!

Sitting across from me, as I gobbled down the wonderful soup and slice after slice of bread smeared with creamy sweet butter, Ma studied me closely. By the time I had finished my fourth slice of bread and was reaching for a fifth, her usually calm eyes were angry and her face was grim.

"Am I eating too much, Ma?"

"Eat it all, child. There's ample bread in the bin. That farmer and his wife did not care for thee well. Thee art thin and worn enough to be a scarecrow. How is it they did not feed thee proper?"

"They were not proper folk," I answered, my mouth crammed, and I began to tell her about them. "It will be hard for you to believe what I say about them, but they were really *wolves*."

That startled her. She sat bolt upright and gave me her full attention. As she listened, she became more and more angered by what she heard.

I reached up over my ear to move my hair aside and uncover the bruises on my neck. Then I quit eating just long enough to show her the other marks on my shoulders and legs.

Gasping at my injuries, she was indignant at my story of harsh treatment. "The farmer's wife wrote regularly that thee were well and happy," she said. "I believed her. I am so sorry."

She looked down into her clasped hands. "About

the poorhouse, child, I had no choice. I knew Mrs. Eddington to be kind, so I left thee in her charge. But — these people — I would not have let thee stay there one moment if I'd known."

"She said you wrote you were glad to get my wages."

"Indeed, the money was needed and welcome. But thee can sew. A seamstress earns wages, too. I would *not* have left thee there," she repeated, her face pale, *"not one second,* if I had known."

Rising, she went directly to the box where she kept her letter paper and pen and ink. "We must act immediately! We must see to it that Mrs. Eddington does not send another girl to them."

"Oh, Ma!" I hadn't thought of that possibility and I was horrified. The girl could be Sally! Living there would kill her. She wasn't terribly strong.

Ma wrote a long, detailed letter that very night, and she put in a message at the end from me to Sally that I was home, at last, and thinking of her. I got to write in a bunch of *X*s for kisses. I did a dozen in a row all neatly lined up.

X   X   X   X   X   X   X   X   X   X   X   X

"They must never abuse another child in Mrs. Eddington's care," Ma said with satisfaction, as she sealed her envelope and slipped it into Grandpap's pouch to carry out when he next took the mail. "Thee had best forget them forever. It is important for thee to put this behind thee and strive not to dwell on it. Think instead on the goodness of people."

Good advice. Good advice but impossible to follow. How I wanted to erase the hunger and the beatings and the meanness!

My whole life afterward, I've done my best to forget the wolves — and Emmeline Sue Smathers — but they return in bad dreams and dark places. I have never escaped them entirely. They taught me about meanness and cruelty in people. Just as the Bunburys taught me about goodness and generosity.

Two months after Ma wrote her letter, Mrs. Eddington answered. Hers was the longest letter I ever saw. Some of it I could read all by myself. The rest Ma read to me, and all of it was so remarkable, I have saved it and I carry it in my Bible wherever I go.

Here it is, Mrs. Eddington's Letter:

My dear Mrs. Shaw,

I thank you for your letter, which unfortunately was delayed several days by our local postmaster's arthritis. He did not get around to sorting the mail till the damp weather cleared.

Two days after Annie ran away, her angry employer appeared here, loud with accusations about Annie's sloth, her dishonesty, her disrespect, and her clumsiness.

He said she couldn't sew and she dropped

the darning egg in the fire, where it was charred.

"I can't believe that. I taught her to sew myself," I said. "She's handy with the needle."

He next said Annie made off with his wife's silver candlesticks.

"That cannot be so. This child comes of Quaker parents. Quakers are honest folk," I told him.

He demanded another mother's helper, at once.

I was not enthusiastic, but Emmeline Sue, a sturdy, tough orphan, who has been troublesome here, wanted to go. "You gave the job to Moses-Poses," she said, "now give it to me. I want a turn." She is three years Annie's senior and can look out better for herself. With misgivings, I let her go along with him.

Emmeline Sue lasted all of two days. Somehow, mysteriously during the second night, the farmer's springhouse caught fire and burned clear to the ground!

During the fire, Emmeline Sue disappeared. The farmer insists she took his money jar with two hundred dollars in it, but I know nothing of that.

I believe that is the last we shall see of him. As for Emmeline Sue, I have reported her missing and hope she will be found. But of all my wards, I believe, she is most capable of surviving on her own. It is unchristian of me, but I feel some relief at her departure.

Please tell Annie that Sally is thriving. Mrs. Aspinwall-Jones, her teacher, has found that she can comfortably read in the *fourth McGuffey Reader*, and she believes Sally may have a natural talent for teaching young children. She has started giving her special tutoring so she can catch up.

Sally sends love to Annie and double the kisses.

X X X X X X X X X X X X
X X X X X X X X X X X X

I am sorry for Annie's hardships and very glad she is with you at home. I shall try to better supervise my girls when I place them outside.

Sincerely,
Sarah Eddington
(Mrs. Crawford Eddington)

"Both thee and Mrs. Eddington speak so badly of this Emmeline Sue," Ma said. "Surely, she is but an unfortunate child."

"She's a terrible bully, Ma. She really picked on me. She made fun of my name and my clothes."

Ma put the tip of her forefinger to my lips to stop me from speaking ill of an absent person. "Yet she has courage. That is admirable," she observed. "Thee must look for the good in others." After a bit, she added, "Perhaps outside the infirmary she will thrive."

I wasn't about to spend any time worrying about Emmeline Sue Smathers. Now I had the fields and the forests and my sisters and brother and Ma and Grandpap, who was gentle and kind, though sort of forgetful and fuzzy in his mind.

I had my life back again!

As usual, something got in the way.

Sewing.

11

MA TRULY HOPED that I'd be a seamstress. It was a ladylike occupation. Mrs. Eddington had trained me in fine needlework, so I could now do quilting, smocking, fagoting, and hemstitching. This impressed Ma, who was skilled with the needle herself. She said I had talent, and she turned more and more of her sewing chores over to me as she went off to do nursing.

This was a talent I didn't care about.

But I tried to do it for her sake. For months and months, I sat sewing most of the daylight hours, obeying Ma. Johnny often came and sat beside me, forlorn, as I stitched away. My sewing brought in a little extra money. Not enough to matter. Not enough to buy groceries.

We were eating mainly out of the garden those days. Though Grandpap kept the deerskin bag filled with bullets, his eyes were weak and he had arthritis, so he couldn't hunt or trap. Sometimes he'd catch a fish, but mostly Ma did the best she could with what we grew. We ate so much turnip stew, I thought my nose was getting to look like a turnip.

I'd sit sewing and thinking about what critters were out there hiding in the bushes, just waiting. I'd think about them every single stitch I took.

The outdoors was calling me, but I had to force myself to stay put. *Sit right there, Annie,* my mind would caution, *and don't you dare give in to stubbornness.*

I held out till one bright, cool morning. Then, just after Ma had gone off on her rounds, I just couldn't stop myself.

I put aside that needle and thread and the camisole I was hemming.

With Johnny helping me, I set to cleaning Pa's rifle. That was a task I had performed, step by step, in my mind five hundred times while I was away.

I worked on the gun for well past an hour, rubbing and greasing and polishing. When the blue barrel was gleaming like a mirror inside and out, I took up the cow horn of gunpowder and prepared to load. I held the metal cap in my hand.

"Level or heaping, Johnny?" I asked.

"Level." His answer was right quick. "Best on the low side of level, eh? Level lacking some?" he suggested hopefully, and he stuck his fingers in his ears. We both fell to laughing at the memory of that first explosion.

"Let's go catch us some dinner," I said, and off we traipsed into the woods.

Paradise was the Ohio woods on that summer morning, no cloud in the sky, ribbons of sunlight gleaming through the trees, all the birds and the forest critters moving quietly about us in the deep, soft green.

"*Avis*," Johnny whispered, proud of his Latin. Quickly, he moved back.

He was right.

Like it was saying "I see you" to my "Peekaboo," a big wild turkey came out of the brush, flapping its wings madly.

Moving my arm in an arc, I raised the gun, and at that moment my eyes saw only the target. My surroundings — forest, sunlight — even Johnny — vanished. My mind moved into a silent world where I was alone with that turkey. I heard nothing, neither the birdsongs nor the wind rustling the leaves. I was enveloped in a vast stillness that I broke with a shot that brought the turkey down.

"Annie," Johnny said with awe, "ain't no one in the whole wide world can shoot like you."

"Probably lotsa folks can."

He shook his head stubbornly.

"You just ain't seen 'em yet."

Just at that minute there was a slight rustle again. Johnny and I narrowed our eyes and scanned the dark green foliage.

"I see tail feathers," he whispered, pointing to a clump of brambles on our right. "Down low on the left near the oak."

I began to reload, taking my time.

"Hurry, Annie," John panicked. "He'll get away."

I didn't speed up.

"Annie?" he pleaded.

"I'm not going to shoot a sitting bird, John. It's too easy and it's not fair."

"What's fair got to do with it?"

"I made up my mind. Every living critter deserves a fair chance." I didn't want to tell him I had spent two years with no chance at all. "I'm going to practice shooting till I can spin around and aim and fire."

John smiled, dazzled by the idea.

Well, by the time we started back many hours later, we had us more than one, more than two — yes, indeed, *three* turkeys. Good-sized.

I couldn't squeeze but one into the game pouch I had slung on my shoulder. So Johnny was hauling the second one along, and I carried my gun and the third.

Walking was slow and hard for us with these heavy birds, even slower because I was beginning to worry about how Ma would receive them.

Just then Johnny said, "We've got enough here for three Thanksgivings, Annie." His saying that made me hopeful.

Surely, surely Ma wouldn't fret at three Thanksgivings' worth of turkey. Still, I dragged my feet.

Grandpap was sitting outdoors whittling when he spotted us moseying along like a wagon train of snails. He stared, pop-eyed. "Where'd you two get them birds?"

"Shot 'em," I said. We were real close, and I could see his eyes counting: one, two, three!

"More'n we need, I guess, Grandpap."

"You *guess*? Why I can't remember the last time we had turkey. You wait right there till your ma sees you." He was real excited. "Susan!" he called. "You got to come out here at once and see a miracle!"

Ma came a-hurrying at his call, but to her it wasn't any miracle. She stopped short and just stood there right by him, silent and looking very serious. When she did speak it was direct to me.

Her words were a sharp disappointment. "Thee abandoned the sewing which was promised . . . ," she started. Then she paused, her eyes on the turkeys.

She did not continue scolding me. Her next words were spoken slow and careful.

"Thee art a good child to provide for us. I thank thee for that. I am grateful for the food." Then she stopped speaking altogether, her eyes sad, her hands clasped before her.

I'd gone so long without praise or caresses or hugs, I really hungered for them.

She did not advance to stroke my hair or touch me or hug me. Her hands remained locked together.

"Son," she said and put out a hand to John. He ran to her and handed her his turkey. She chucked him under the chin fondly and sent him off to wash his sweaty face and dirty hands.

"Ma?" I remained standing there. "I am real good with the gun."

"Thee must conquer this stubbornness and spend time sewing."

"But Ma —"

"Shooting is no fit pastime for a young girl. It is unseemly . . ."

Mrs. Honoria had used that very word about girls running. Yet I'd had to run to escape. I'd had to run to get to the train. To exist.

If a person has to run to be free, how can that not be *seemly*?

And now, my hunting was helping all of us to survive. Why was it unseemly?

"What does it matter if it brings us food? If John could shoot, he would."

"He might do it with my blessing. Thee art a girl."

"I'm mighty careful. Ask him."

She shook her head. "I do not doubt thee nor blame thee. And I am glad for the food. Yet . . ." She shrugged and didn't finish.

I carried my birds into the kitchen. I didn't feel like shouting, "Turkey ho! Turkey ho!" this time.

I felt more like ducking my head and crying.

It took a long time — years and years — for me to understand Ma.

She needed the game I shot to feed our family. She never turned it down or wasted any of it. She sent extra meat to needy neighbors.

But she longed for me to be a proper girl. Proper girls were always ladylike, she believed. Proper girls *did not ever shoot*.

That was the rule.

I thought it was a silly rule.

I still think so.

Silly because I can't see any reason to stop a person who has a talent just because that person is a girl.

Ma herself was the one who first named mine. A shooting talent.

Who says boys are the only ones allowed to have talents and use them?

12

TIME BEGAN TO WHISK BY now that I was again roaming about outdoors in North Star. I continued to do some sewing for pay when I'd a mind to, but I hated doing it. Me and John hiked and hunted and trapped together.

Ma never really came around, never smiled on what I did or embraced me when saying thanks — but she *did* say thanks each time, and she never once forbade me to use the gun.

Silently, she received what John and I brought home, and she cooked and cured and smoke-dried it. And we ate it.

I started to give John the shooting lessons I'd promised him.

We practiced every day and he became a fair shot at sitting game. He couldn't seem to hit a moving target. I couldn't explain how I did it. It was just my eyes; they were true. He understood that he was never to use the gun on his own.

Mornings we'd rise at sunup and go into the woods and set snares or empty the filled traps, and we'd hunt us some supper.

I took to wearing a sack over my linsey dress to save

it from the thorns and cockleburs. Each sack had its own smell, so some days I'd smell of coffee beans and other days I'd smell of flour. I had Pa's old cap to shade my eyes, and on my feet I wore heavy metal-tipped boots — big for me but Ma said I'd grow into 'em. (I never did!)

We'd bring back what we caught, and we'd clean it and dress it.

I kept practicing my shooting.

I got so fast I could twirl around *twice* and then just raise the gun and fire. Hardly had to aim after a while. That rifle obeyed me as if it was part of me.

Well, as I got better and better at hunting, we had more and more to eat — and lots left over.

All the while, Ma and Grandpap were worrying themselves sick over the mortgage. Two hundred dollars! They were barely managing.

We'd a'had no place to live if they lost the farm. As the end of each month drew near, they were filled with fear that there wouldn't be enough money coming in to pay the bank. Our sewing money, Ma's salary from her nursing, and Grandpap's wages as mailman didn't stretch far enough.

One day I had me a bold idea. As usual, it came out of nowhere, and once it came it wouldn't go away. I decided to try it out on Grandpap first, because he was much easier than Ma.

I cornered him outside one evening when he drove up in the mail wagon. "Grandpap, you think some store in Greenville might be interested in having fresh birds for sale? I'm shooting far more than we can use."

He thought about it. "Worth a try," he said.

"Maybe I could ride in with you one day and ask."

"Next mail day, you come along with me and I'll interduce you to Charlie Katzenberger. He runs the big general store."

"First I got to ask Ma if she'll let me."

"That'll be harder than askin' Charlie," Grandpap said, shaking his head. "I can tell you now, she won't like it one bit."

How right he was.

"It's not fitting," she said, "for a girl."

"I could ask *for* Annie," Grandpap offered hopefully. "I could talk about the birds and just sorta mention to Charlie about her shootin'."

"No," I said stubbornly.

He meant well, but he wasn't too good at business. He said so many times himself. That's how he got cheated out of his farm money.

"Grandpap, thanks just the same. I'm not ashamed of the truth. Ma" — I turned to her — "please let me. I understand about the mortgage. This might get us some money. Please, let me try."

Ma bit her lower lip. "Men will mock thee. Thee will be insulted and left with hurt feelings and pain."

"I'm not afraid. After the wolves, I know I'm strong."

"Susan," Grandpap said, "we are in terrible money trouble. If the child can help . . ."

I figured I might as well speak my whole piece. No

sense stopping half way. I turned back to Grandpap. "Does Mr. Katzenberger buy furs, too? I got a pile of pelts . . ."

Grandpap shook his head.

I was mighty disappointed.

"But Frenchy LaMotte, down the street from Charlie, he deals in furs. And guns and traps and lantern oil — all huntin' stuff. Started out as a hunter himself up in Canada. Don't know if he'd buy from a girl . . ."

He stopped and waited, maybe hoping I'd say, Go ahead, tell them you're the hunter, but I didn't say that.

"Can I show him my furs?"

"Don't see why not. Can't hurt."

"Nothing wrong with girls," I said. "We're half of God's creatures."

"You just tell Frenchy that." Grandpap laughed. "He'll appreciate that."

"A hunters' store is a rowdy place. It's not fit for womenfolk — or girls," Ma said. "It's a man's store."

"I seen women in there along with their men," Grandpap spoke right up. "Many times. I'll go along with the child, Susan. Frenchy's a good man. A bit rough on the outside is all. Nothin' to fret about."

No more was said then. Ma hadn't agreed, but she hadn't forbidden me to go, either. That was her Quaker way, to leave me to consult my conscience and make my own decision.

Afterward, I heard the two of them talking softly by the fireside long into the night. I heard that word *mort-*

gage, mortgage, mortgage whispered over and over, fearfully.

Mortgage is the second worst word in the English language.

The first worst word is *death*.

Grandpap carried the mail twice a week.

Three days afterward, true to his promise, he came to me. "Can you be ready early tomorrow morning? I'm goin' to town and we can conduct your business."

"How about Ma?"

"She still don't want you to go, but she won't say you nay."

All that day was spent hunting, and then John helped me till late into the night getting everything ready. Together we cleaned and dressed a dozen grouse and quail and strung them and wrapped them in damp marsh grass to keep them fresh.

I chose the finest pelts I had — raccoon, squirrel, and muskrat — and tied them in a neat bundle to show this Frenchy LaMotte.

Ma went about her cooking and gardening briskly and didn't discuss the goings on, but when I woke up and saw my best dress laid out on my bed all clean and freshly ironed, I knew she was saying, in her own way, that it was all right.

I'd filled the tin basin with water and washed myself all over, most particular, with soap last thing before I had gone to sleep.

Not having any other shoes, I had to wear the old boots. Rubbing tallow on them didn't improve them much, but the rest of me was dressed up special in my new green frock.

I worked hard brushing my hair, getting it ready to be combed and neatly braided. I went to the mirror. A small, thin girl with blue-gray eyes and thick, curly brown hair looked back at me. I wanted so much to look nice, but I feared I looked plain.

Suddenly Ma came in, her two hands, rolled into fists, side-by-side holding something. She put her fists out for me to open. In them was a lovely, matching, green hair ribbon to work into my plait. She hefted my hair in her hands and began to braid it, something she hadn't done in years.

"The ribbon's grogram," she said. "A special weave. I bought it back East a long, long time ago. Such thick lovely hair deserves a bright ribbon."

When she was finished braiding, she came around and took my chin in her hand and gazed at me. "Thee art mighty pretty, child," she said.

The first time she'd ever said such a thing to me!

I didn't feel a bit plain after that. I felt beautiful. And filled with hope.

Looking me over carefully one last time, she straightened my skirt and then smoothed my hair. "If Jacob were alive it would not be necessary for thee to do this," she said, sighing.

I kissed her cheek.

Once we were in the wagon and about to drive off,

she cautioned Grandpap, "Stay by her every single minute and keep careful watch over her."

"Yes'm, I will. I promise."

Her last words were carried after us on the wind. "Remember, she is but a child. Protect her."

He looked at me and chuckled, greatly pleased with himself. "Ain't every day old Joseph Shaw gets to pertect the best shot in Darke County."

13

RIDING INTO GREENVILLE in the daytime was mighty exciting!

First we passed a sawmill making an earsplitting clatter; next, a blacksmith working at his forge, with giant flames shooting up all around; then there was a great flour mill grinding away.

Lots of folks were walking about on the streets dressed in what looked like their Sunday clothes, many of the ladies in bonnets and the men in jackets.

The one particular street we rode on, the main road, was called Broadway; it was rightly named because it *was* broad. Both sides of Broadway were lined with buildings so close they looked to be leaning on each other, houses and shops, hardware and fur trading, and even a tavern.

"Grandpap," I said, "a person could buy pretty much everything he needed to live, right here in Greenville."

"Guess so. But there's fifty times more of it in the city, in Cincinnati. More'n fifty. A hundred times more."

Cincinnati was where my sister Lydia and her hus-

band, Joe Stein, lived. I couldn't even imagine such a
grand place.

"Your important business comes first, Annie, then
the mail," Grandpap said, pulling in front of a big
store with shining clean windows. He got out of the
wagon and started inside, me trailing behind him carrying the game.

Katzenberger's store, to my eye, was a marvel, and
I set out to memorize every detail to tell about back
home.

On the floor stood sacks of coffee that gave off rich
smells, and more sacks of sugar and flour, and boxes
and crates all around held all kinds of groceries and
household stuff and dry goods.

There was a whole crate just of different kinds of fly
swatters!

I'd never seen so many wares and so much costly
store food in one place. *Where does it all come from?* I
wondered. *How do they get it way out here?*

There was a long wooden meat counter, and above
it high up on the wall ropes of sausages were braided
around and around a peg.

Right beside the meat counter was a giant pickle
barrel that smelled spicy and vinegary, and past that
stood a shiny, all-glass case with cheeses in huge balls
and blocks. Some of the cheeses were funny colored
and looked old and jagged like rocks.

Tobacco and snuff added their nasty smells to the
place, and in the rear there was the kerosene vat with

a tap so folks could fill their own cans and carry them away.

A stout man behind the counter was busy sorting money in a large metal box. He was blond-haired and had a large stomach and a rosy face; he looked as if he spent a lot of time eating his own cheese and sausages.

Grandpap waited till he had finished all his counting, locked the box and put it on a shelf underneath, hung the key on its heavy silver chain around his neck, and wiped his hands on the big white apron he wore.

All these different steps took almost forever.

My leg muscles were cramped with eagerness to step forward, to get going. But, of course, I didn't move. I barely breathed.

"Charlie," Grandpap spoke up at last, "this here is Annie. She's my wife Susan's daughter and she's come all the way to town with me and the mail today to show you somethin' special."

"Hello. Little Miss . . ." Mr. Katzenberger looked at me questioningly, his eyes resting on the bulky swamp-grass bundle in my hands. "What have you there?"

I didn't say a word.

I just set down that whole passel of birds and unwrapped them and spread them out over his meat counter.

"I would like to sell these to you," I said.

This seemed to confuse him.

"Fine birds," he nodded, not knowing what else to

say. He looked up at us, then back down at the birds lying there. "Who bagged them?"

"I did, sir," I said.

He laughed loud at that. "That's a good one." Then he nudged Grandpap with his elbow. "C'mon, Joe. Where'd they come from? Did you find 'em in a post-box?"

Grandpap was extremely perturbed. He fidgeted on his feet, not looking Mr. Katzenberger in the eye. "I shot 'em," he mumbled, at last. "I had me a good day."

"You?" Again the grocer hooted with laughter. "Come on, Joe, we're old friends. We both know with them eyes you couldn't sight a buffalo knockin' on your front door!" A fit of coughing and laughing took him so bad he had to dig out his handkerchief and blow his nose and wipe the tears away.

All this laughing and ragging Grandpap got my dander up.

"I shot them, sir," I said again. "Grandpap only lied to help me sell them to you, but *I shot them.*"

He didn't pay me much mind. "Come on, Joe, tell me who really bagged these birds."

Grandpap pointed at me with his chin. "That youngun did it."

"I can hardly believe that . . ."

Now there were tears in my eyes. I did my best not to let him see.

Ma was right. They'd never treat me fair. These were the wages of stubbornness. And it did hurt.

I reached over to gather up my birds and take them home with me.

"Whoa! Hold up there a minute, young lady. Don't be in such a hurry," Mr. Katzenberger said. He put out a hand to stop me. "It's just very hard for me to believe my own ears. Now, tell me one last time, who did this hunting?"

"I did, sir," I said, staring him right back in the eyes.

"All right," he said. "I believe you, and I'm sorry I laughed."

Then he bent over to examine the birds more closely. He could see what a clean shot I was.

"Well!" he said; and, liking the sound of it, he repeated it five more times. "Well, well, well, well, well!" He rubbed his hands together, palm against palm. "And you're here to do business with Charlie Katzenberger?"

"Yes, sir!"

"I'll give you ten cents a bird. No, because they sell better in pairs, I'll give you twenty-five cents a brace. How's that for an offer?"

I didn't say a word. My face just broke into a bigger grin than a jack o'lantern on All Saints' Eve.

"Can you bring me more of these, regular-like?" Mr. Katzenberger wanted to know.

"Grandpap, here, can carry them in with the mail. Can't you, Grandpap?"

"You bet." He chuckled. "Every mail day."

Mr. Katzenberger went and lifted his metal money box back up. "You swear you shot them yourself?" he asked me one more time.

"My mother does not permit me to swear, sir, but I did shoot them myself."

"Good enough for me."

He took the key from around his neck and unlocked the box and began to count out the coins for me on top of the glass counter, each one jingling like a tiny silver bell. There was a pile of them, more than I had ever held before.

My hand, when I reached to pick them up, was trembling. I let the last coin lie there. "Can I buy some sweets for my brother and sisters?" I asked.

"My treat." Mr. Katzenberger immediately picked up a tin scoop and filled a small paper sack with a wonderful mixture of the candy he had in the big jars behind the counter.

"No, sir. I'll be glad to pay."

"Now, now. I won't hear of it. We're in business together."

Charlie Katzenberger reached for the remaining coin and put it in my hand and gently closed my fingers over it. "But I should know my business partner's name, now shouldn't I? Annie?"

"Mozee," I said, surprising Grandpap. I wouldn't use the old name ever again. "Annie Mozee."

Phoebe Anne Moses was gone forever.

Mr. Katzenberger put out his hand and we shook

hands. "Now, Annie Mozee," he said, "you're a market hunter."

I felt proud.

"I'm off to interduce her to Frenchy LaMotte," Grandpap said. "She don't limit herself to shootin' birds. No sirree."

Mr. Katzenberger hurried to the door and held it open for me. He stood in the doorway looking after us, amazed at all that had taken place, and most of all that I was a girl.

I could tell because the last thing he said to Grandpap was, "That's quite a *girl* you've got there. Quite a *girl.*"

14

FRENCHY LAMOTTE was different.

From the minute he saw me and I saw him, we were friends.

Just like with Sally.

Sometimes in life, if you're real lucky, you'll meet a person and a signal will go right off in your mind: *Bang!* This is a true friend.

Mostly it doesn't happen between two people if one is grown and the other is still a child — Frenchy was much older'n me — but it happened!

Bang!

Grandpap and I walked into this little store crowded with furs and traps and harnesses and lanterns and guns and all sorts of other hunting stuff piled up together every which way. Good thing Ma wasn't along or she'd have hauled me right out of there. It didn't look fit; it looked disorderly. Ma liked things real neat.

A bunch of men were standing around the wood-stove over in the corner having a loud discussion to do with roads. It was all about the main road and the railroad and goods and transport.

Standing in the doorway unnoticed, Grandpap and I listened in. Near as I could figure, the crowd was divided: half of them felt the county needed to get another railroad — the trains coming in four times a day weren't near enough to carry folks and goods.

The other side was all het up about having a good plank road built from Greenville clear to Cincinnati — eighty miles — that would make better road travel and transport.

It was a good-natured argument with a whole lot of laughing and teasing. Every once in a while, a man would interrupt what he was saying and spit tobacco juice into the spittoon. The talk kept spinning round and round. A robber could've easily sneaked out with the store's goods and those men arguing wouldn't have noticed. Least of all the store's owner, who was right in the middle of the argument.

"That's him." Grandpap pointed out Frenchy, a strong-looking little man with red hair and a frizzy red beard. He wasn't good-looking, but he smiled a lot, and he'd win the prize for fastest and loudest talker in Greenville, easy.

He waved his hands about and thumped on the cracker barrel and stabbed whoever he was arguing with in the chest with his forefinger when he was making a point.

Watching, I wondered how anyone could care so much about roads or railroads. Later on, I came to know that Frenchy cared about everything. That was just the way he was.

His speech was very strange to my ears. He said words a different way from anyone else, and I had to listen real close to understand. It wasn't Latin, it was twisted English.

Frenchy LaMotte was on the side of the railroad. Once I listened to him and sorted out what he said, I was sure he was right and I sided with the railroad, too. A man that felt so strong about something that he couldn't stand or keep still had to be right.

As soon as he looked up and noticed us, he put out his hand, fingers spread wide to shush the others. "One minute, *mes amis*. A young lady has come in."

"Aah, what have you there?" he asked, coming toward us, his eyes on my thick pile of pelts.

"Well, Frenchy," Grandpap started, "this here is my wife Susan's daughter, Annie." He was having trouble explaining.

I could see how uncomfortable he was. Charlie Katzenberger had given us such a hard time, and that was with no one else listening. In here in front of all these men, Grandpap didn't want to seem a fool.

"I've brought some furs to trade," I interrupted, coming quickly to the point.

"You have, Mademoiselle . . . ?"

"Mozee," I said.

"Ah, Mademoiselle Mozee."

My new name was as beautiful as a song the way he said it.

Without another word — like he was used to having twelve-year-old girl-hunters bring him furs — he put his hand out for them, and I gladly gave them to him.

"Thank you." Carrying them over to the big wooden

table that served as his counter, he cleared a place and
spread them out and began to examine them very carefully. He studied each one and then turned it over,
neat as a page in a book, and moved on to the next.

"Who did the shooting?" he asked.

"Me."

"You shot all?"

"Every single one."

He scratched his head. "*Mes amis,*" he called to the
men standing around up front, "come and see."

They came and looked over the furs and mumbled
and shook their heads. "Pretty sharp shootin'," a tall
older man finally said, and then he poked the young
man next to him. "When you gonna shoot that clean,
son?" There were some loud laughs and snorts at that.

I was too embarrassed to look up, so I kept my eyes
on the floor. Frenchy shooed them all away to the
front of the store again, and then he came back.

"Who taught you to shoot, Mademoiselle?"

"No one. I just practice a lot."

"She's a natural." Grandpap grinned with pride.

"You're a fine shot, Annie Mozee."

"Thank you. Can I trade the furs for powder and
bullets and stuff, Mr. LaMotte?"

"*Mais non!*" he said sternly.

I didn't understand French, but I knew that meant
no.

Then a mischievous smile lit his face. "Only if you
call me Frenchy. That is my name."

Grandpap let out a big sigh of relief.

Frenchy gave me plenty of powder and bullets in payment for my pelts. "I will pay some cash, too," he offered, counting out a few coins. My pocket was heavy with money.

"Can I send more with Grandpap when he brings the mail?"

"*Mais oui.* With him or come yourself. You and your furs are always welcome."

Frenchy — carrying my parcels — walked us out to where our wagon was hitched. He waited till Grandpap loaded up and we were all set, and then he put his hand to his brow and saluted me. I saluted right back and turned to watch him take the steps back into his store two at a time. Probably he was in a big hurry to argue for railroads.

He had not mocked me or hurt my feelings. He'd hardly noticed that I was a girl. It didn't matter.

I was so happy that I made up my mind to bring him some fresh game birds as a gift next time I came to Greenville.

He appreciated my talent.

I'd made me a friend.

15

AFTER I HELPED Grandpap load up the mail in the wagon, we rode out of town silently, each of us thinking our own private thoughts. It had been a powerful exciting day.

Finally, I spoke up. "Grandpap, if you'll help deliver the birds and the furs regular, we'll have some money coming in."

He didn't answer for a long time. He was making funny sounds, which he kept trying to choke down. I think he was crying. Then he said, in a real husky voice, "Annie, girl, I wouldn'a thought it possible, but I believe it now, and I'll help you any way I can."

"But Ma . . ." I said sadly, remembering.

"She is how she is. Can't change. She understands we need the money. You show her what Charlie and Frenchy paid you for your birds and furs. It won't make her happy, but your ma is strong. She's hadda be."

And, again, he was exactly right.

When we got home, I went right in and showered the money into the sewing basket in Ma's lap. It covered all the spools of thread. "It's all for you," I said. "I earned it hunting."

She looked down at the pile of coins. "I'm grateful," she said, biting her lip. "I'm truly grateful."

And that's all she said.

We never talked about it after that.

When I opened the sack of sweets and passed it back and forth under the children's noses just to show what I'd got, they flung themselves on me and kissed me and hugged me.

Their joy was mine, too.

That evening after dinner was candy time.

First, Ma took a peppermint and Grandpap a horehound. We children decided to try all the different kinds, so I made a little pile of candies in front of each of us — John, Hulda, Emily, and me: horehound, peppermint, lemon drop, rock candy, and a sarsaparilla stick.

I thought the lemon drop was best, maybe because it reminded me of Mrs. Honoria, but the others voted for rock candy. Except for Johnny. He loved the sarsaparilla stick because it was so big.

Mr. Katzenberger had been big-hearted: we had several nights' worth. How sweet it all was!

And so I became Annie Mozee, a market hunter. Every day except the Sabbath, no matter the weather, excepting for blizzards, I'd set out at daybreak — mostly with John by my side — and we'd wander the open fields and the woods looking for game: rabbits, ruffed grouse, pigeons, wild ducks, and ever so many quail.

Whatever I shot, I'd clean and gut, and then I'd send them off to Charlie Katzenberger. Mostly Grandpap took care of things for me, but every once in a while I'd ride into Greenville and talk to Charlie, then visit with Frenchy.

When my gun needed repair because the sight seemed a little off, I trusted him with it and he did a fine repair job. The rifle was good as new.

I was delighted to be free in my own favorite place — the outdoors. I picked berries and nuts and ate to my heart's content. I tramped over miles of countryside till I knew it all intimately.

My hunting was bringing money in and we were paying off the bank.

It was such a joyful time in my life, I forgot all about unlucky 13.

Then one night Grandpap came back with the money and a message. "Charlie says you got to ease up a bit. You're shooting more game birds than he can sell in Greenville."

I was scared. "I better talk to him. I'll ride in with you next time, Grandpap."

I got some pelts ready for Frenchy and prepared two beautiful quail as a gift, and since I needed advice I decided to visit with him first.

After I gave Frenchy my gift of the birds, I told him about the message Charlie had sent. "I need to sell what I shoot, Frenchy. Ma and Grandpap count on it."

"Mademoiselle Annie, I will go with you to talk to Charlie. He is my good friend."

By the time we got to the general store, Frenchy had come up with an idea. Ideas flew out of Frenchy's head as easily as seeds from a dandelion.

Here was his thought: Charlie might send the extra birds on with the mail carrier to Cincinnati! Mr. John Frost, who managed the grand Bevis House Hotel, was always pleased to buy fresh game. Frenchy knew that from his own hunting days.

"A wonderful idea!" Charlie exclaimed. "Those hotel customers will appreciate your birds shot clean through the head. Then they can eat without worrying about biting into shot pellets. Leave it to me, Annie. I'll set it up."

He did.

Mr. Frost bought all I could shoot. He sent word that his customers enjoyed the fowl immensely.

"Eeemensely!" Frenchy loved the word.

I did, too. I was fourteen years old and life was immensely good. I didn't think it could get any better than it was.

Till one remarkable Friday morning.

"Take a holiday today from hunting," Ma said to me, soon as I woke. "We're going into town to the bank. And thee must come along." She looked myste-rious.

"Aw, Ma! John and I planned to hike —"

"Thee *must* come along," she repeated.

Oddly, Grandpap, who usually sided with me, stepped in here. "Listen to your mother," he said. Then he was all smiles. "Today we pay off the mort-gage, Annie. And it's thanks to you."

Gladly, I took a holiday and went along to the bank!

I watched Ma take the last payment from her bag and hand it over. First, she counted, then the banker counted again, and then there was ever so much name-signing on important papers.

Everybody signed: Ma, Grandpap, the banker, and then the two witnesses who were brought in.

Everybody except me (even though I could sign my name real good by then). I couldn't be a witness, the banker explained, because I was a minor. That meant I was too young.

"Seems to me her name belongs on the paper, too, somewhere," Grandpap said, and Ma nodded agree-ment.

"No harm in that," the banker agreed.

Minor Witness, he printed in a clean bottom corner, and I signed, too.

I couldn't read the complicated parts or understand much of what was going on — the banker in his black suit reminded me of the Reverend Sylvester, even though Ma said later on that *debtee* and *mortgagee* and *creditor* and *negotiable instruments* were just proper business words.

Not Latin.

English.

When the banker finally stood up, I knew the bewildering business talk was done.

He walked around his immense desk and handed Ma the mortgage paper with silver seals and red stamps and all our signatures — even mine — on it, and he said, "Felicitations, Mr. and Mrs. Shaw. Now you just transport that mortgage home and incinerate it so it's gone forever."

I'd half a mind to ask him if he favored cucumber sandwiches, but I didn't have the courage. I looked around. Sure enough, in one corner of his office stood a big, black, rolled-up umbrella in an iron umbrella stand. I just knew he would have one.

On the bank steps outside, Ma tucked that mortgage paper in her bag, and then she drew me to her and kissed me on the forehead and said, "Thee art a fine daughter. I am thankful. I could not ask for better, Annie."

I had never been happier in my whole life.

She'd called me Annie, at last.

16

I am almost up to the happily ever after part!

It was Pa's old, long-barreled cap-and-ball Pennsylvania rifle that did it.

It allowed us to live peaceable and content, on our farm in North Star, through my fourteenth and fifteenth years.

With me market hunting, there was regular money coming in. Ma gave up her community nursing and stayed at home.

I began to earn enough so that we could make improvements on the farm.

Knowing how much Ma loved fruit trees and all the preserving and baking they allowed, I set up a surprise. After doing secret errands in Greenville with Grandpap, I came home one evening and began to tease her. "I know you'd be plumb against having some more apple and pear trees in our orchard, wouldn't you, Ma?"

She was startled. "Against?"

"I mean, it'd be a lot of trouble and work, caring for extra young trees. You've got enough to do."

Her eyes shone very bright. "I can't imagine anything I'd be more *for*. An orchard would make me feel *grand!*" She went to stand in the doorway and gaze out at her few beloved trees. "Like a queen." She smiled at me. "Like Queen Victoria on the Earl Grey Tea calendar."

Charlie Katzenberger had given me that calendar, which now hung near our hearth, as a gift. The Queen was all ruffles and ribbons and petticoats, stiff and starchy-looking.

Did Queen Victoria have fruit trees?

Yes, I decided, *she must have; there is nothing queens don't have.*

"Well, Queen Susan — Grandpap and I brought six apple and six pear saplings from town."

Her smile was bright enough to light the world.

So we planted the new young trees. We could hardly wait for springtime when we'd have showers of blossoms, their sweet scent all around. In bloom, our trees were very beautiful, and soon enough they began to bear fruit.

"We need to make our garden bigger," I announced another night, after I returned from Greenville where I'd traded a bunch of pelts and had had a serious talk with Frenchy.

He was always giving me good advice.

Today he'd said, "Mademoiselle Mozee, you will see that the more you plant the more you have. The bigger the garden the better."

"What shall I plant, Frenchy?"

"That depends on what you like to eat."

"Everything."

He raised his eyebrows. "That garden will be *formidable*." He laughed and stretched his arms out as wide as they would go. "For you must plant everything."

So I ordered packets and packets of seeds: vegetable seeds and melon seeds and even some flower seeds, because Ma loved the bright colors of blossoms. We all worked together digging and hoeing and seeding and then, later on, weeding.

Then we got more animals, a fine roan horse and some chickens, and two more cows that soon gave us baby calves.

I used to gallop that horse through the pasture, afternoons, with the greatest pleasure. I got to be pretty good on horseback and even tried a few easy tricks, hanging this way and that and standing and twirling.

Hulda, Emily, and John would sit and watch me ride around, and they'd clap their hands like I was a show. I'd jump off the horse and curtsy to them. We had fun!

"If only we had a springhouse," Ma said wistfully, one hot summer night, "our milk would stay much cooler, and, in winter, we could store our potatoes and apples."

"We *will* have a springhouse," I declared promptly. Grandpap Shaw was all for it, so we built us one right close to our cabin over our brook — a *bigger, better one* than the one the wolves had and that Emmeline Sue had burned down. I made sure of that. I even painted it white so it wouldn't look anything like their shabby old brown one, and I planted flowers all around it.

The white paint prettied it up and the flowers were lovely, but the disguise didn't work.

Every time I carried a pail of milk to it, the scary old ghost crept up and walked right alongside me. *"Lummox! You water the ground with my milk!"* A boot was raised to kick me cruelly in the leg. *"I am not payin' good wages for a cripple."*

The memory made me tremble. So I gave up carrying the milk and let others do that chore.

We were a pretty happy family. Ma kept house, planting, gardening, and sewing, which were the tasks she liked best to do in the whole world.

My married older sisters, Lydia, Elizabeth, and Sarah Ellen, were doing fine. Though they were far away, they sent word often with travelers and they wrote letters and Ma wrote to them regular.

John was becoming quite a good marksman, though he never really developed the love for shooting that I had.

Emily and Hulda were growing fast. They weren't going to turn out to be hunters like me. They fancied their dolls and sewing and gardening.

And one day, a wonderful letter came from the county poorhouse. It was from Sally in her own hand. The script was clear, though the letters were kind of big:

Dear Annie,

I am writing to tell you my good news. Our schoolmistress, Mrs. Aspinwall-Jones and her husband, who have been so kind to me, are leaving to travel through the Far West, opening schools in small towns. They asked me to go with them. Never having any child of their own, they want to adopt me!

Since I have no family and have grown very fond of them, I said yes at once. (Yes! Yes! Yes!)

Mrs. Eddington said yes, too. She thinks she has the gift of prophecy. "Didn't I name you Sally *Jones*?" she's asked me a dozen times. "You already bear their name."

Well, only half their name, but I didn't argue.

Annie, my heart is full of joy. When you brought the *McGuffey Reader* back for me and gave me your place at school, you gave me what I wanted most. A mother and a father.

I have kin now, too. I will always remember you no matter how far away we travel, and I hope your life is happy.

> Ever your friend-sister,
> Sally

I read that letter over and over, admiring Sally's script along with what she had to say. I was so glad she had her happily ever after. This is the other letter I carry in my Bible.

*   *   *

I began again to try to learn to read and write — really learn, with Ma's help. Every afternoon she taught reading, writing, and arithmetic to the young ones. But I had special trouble learning, so after supper she'd call study time, and she'd come and sit with me.

I tried to sound out words. I'd point to each word with my finger, and if I got stuck she would prompt me. I was not an apt student — John could already read and write much better than I could — but Ma was patient and she tried to comfort me.

"Thee art very smart, Annie," she'd say frequently. "Something stops thee from learning."

We worked with the family Bible. It was easy reading familiar passages like "The Lord is my shepherd." I could guess *shepherd*, even though it was a hard word, because I knew the verse.

The trouble was reading new words, long hard ones that I'd never heard before. "The heavens declare the glory of God; and the firmament showeth his handiwork. . . ."

How I wished I had *McGuffey* with its little stories and poems about children who tried hard and did well. It was real easy reading.

I did have a slate and chalk to practice my letters and spelling.

"My hand will guide thee," Ma said, placing my hand first over her own, then under her own, as she tried to help me learn to shape my letters gracefully. That didn't seem to work.

"Like this," she'd say, and she'd carefully trace out a letter, first capital, then small.

"Like this," I'd say, imitating her, but my handwriting was all chicken scratches.

We'd laugh together, and I'd keep on practicing. I'd follow her letters, over and over, trying to get that delicate slant she had. I worked on my writing, but it was slow going.

Now that I could read a bit, I began to puzzle out all the family names written in the front of the Bible, and that was when I made the first promise.

I said to myself, *When I am grown up and can write well, I will change all those names in our Bible.* No more Moses! *Mozee is our name.*

I didn't dare mention this out loud. I only talked about it in the dark of night, to Sally, far away. She would understand. Only Sally knew how deep "Moses-Poses" cut into my heart.

Johnny and I, when we were out hunting, would often go by the little cemetery on the other side of the woods east of our house. Pa was buried there. And Mary Jane.

If I saw some pretty wildflowers, Queen Anne's lace, or daisies or day lilies, I'd start picking a bouquet, and that was always the signal for Johnny to slow up till he was creeping like a turtle as we came near. He inched his feet along. He wasn't keen on cemeteries.

"You go on ahead," I'd tell him. "I'll catch up with you at the brook."

"Why are you going in there, again, Annie?" he'd ask each time.

"Pa's in there, and Mary Jane. Just want to be near them a bit."

I'd brush away the twigs and leaves and rubble on the two graves, put my flowers down nicely, and then stand there awhile. By my fifteenth year, when I was able to read the names on the stones easily, I made the second promise.

"Pa and Mary Jane, I will buy you fine new gravestones one day. They'll be smooth and shiny, not rough and chipped like these."

I came out all fired up and told John my plan, and he said, "Nice new stones are a good idea, Annie. I hope you can do it."

"Oh, I'll do it. Just you wait. And the stones'll say 'Jacob Mozee R.I.P.' and 'Mary Jane Mozee R.I.P.' "

"They better not," John said, "because Mozee is not their name."

" 'Tis so. It's my name now and their name, too. Moses is an ugly name."

His face was very red. "It's my birth name."

"We've got to get rid of it, John. Forever."

"Not me, Annie. I'm keeping it. John Moses" — He poked his own chest with his forefinger — "that's me."

"Then you'll be the only one."

He wouldn't budge. "My name stays as it is, always. Don't you *ever ever ever* dare try to touch it."

Talk about stubborn.

"All right, Johnny. You do what you want with your name. But I'm taking care of the rest of them."

We had always been best friends, John and I, and we stayed that way, 'cept about this. We didn't let it break us up, but it caused hurt between us. He was very angry with me — and he carried that name-anger in his heart.

It's been a great sadness to me.

17

My shooting skill began to gain me respect. But it took a while.

One favorite way to spend a nice afternoon, out on the prairie, was at a shooting match. The menfolk would organize the event and shoot, and the women and children would watch.

They'd set up a target in a big open field — sometimes just a nail in the center of a board. "Hit the nail on the head and win the big prize!" the announcer would call over and over. Every man and boy would try.

I watched, hungering for a turn.

In November, down the road quite a-ways from us, the big event was always the turkey shoot. There'd be a bunch of cutout brown-paper turkeys with crayoned heads, each with a tiny glass-button eye pasted on. One turkey-target for each contestant. You had to aim true and try to get him in the head.

At the end of the shoot, the judges would compare all the paper targets, and the cleanest shot won.

"Shoot Tom in the head and take him home for dinner!" the announcer would keep repeating.

Girls, of course, didn't try. Never. There wasn't any rule saying they couldn't. There didn't need to be a rule. Everybody knew girls didn't know how to shoot.

After a morning of setting our traps in the woods, John and I hitched a ride with Grandpap to watch the turkey shoot. No one else at home was interested; Ma was not one for watching shooting, and Emily and Hulda wouldn't go near it. After leaving us off, Grandpap had to go about delivering the mail, or else he would've stayed.

Walking to the shooting field from the road, John started coaxing me for the trillionth time. "Come on, Annie, ask 'em if you can shoot, too."

"They'll only laugh, Johnny. Shooting contests are not for girls."

"You can beat any one of them, Annie. I know you can."

"Maybe so. But I don't want them making fun of me. We don't need their old turkeys. We'll get our own."

"It's not the turkey. It's the fairness of it." John stuck out his lower lip. "If you're the best shot, they *have* to let you try." He was really distressed.

"They don't *have* to do anything, John. They make the rules."

"You're the one told me every living critter deserves a fair chance. Even a bird. Isn't a girl as good as a bird?"

"Hard to say. Girls can't fly."

He stuck his tongue out at me.

I thought it over. I wanted so much to be in the contest. But I was a coward.

That is, Phoebe Anne Moses was a coward. But Annie Mozee was different.

"All right, Johnny, I'll try. I'll ask if I can shoot."

Then panic set in. "But what if they let me and I don't win?"

"You'll win," he said, and he started leaping up high and making loud war whoops.

The man in charge was just setting the first paper turkey in place on the target.

I walked straight up to him before I could lose my nerve.

"I'd like to try in the shooting match if it'd be all right," I said quietly.

He squinted at me kind of funny as if I was talking Latin, which he didn't understand. "Eh? What'dja say? What's that, girl?"

"I'd like to shoot if it's all right, sir."

"Shoot? Didja say *shoot*?"

Thinking that maybe he didn't hear so good, I began to nod my head. John followed my lead. The two of us just stood there, our heads bobbing up and down like corks on water.

"Shoot," the man repeated, making sure he'd understood. "Well, I can't rightly say."

Staring at my gun resting on my shoulder, he swallowed one big swallow and pulled his earlobe. "Hmmm. Let me talk to t'others." He walked over to consult with some men huddling in one corner of the field.

Once he started explaining and pointing, they all turned and looked at me curious, like I was a two-headed calf. Then they talked some more among themselves.

Finally, he came walking back. "Can't see why not," he said. "You git to shoot, too. First girl ever. No fee." He turned his attention to seeing that the target was set up.

Standing nearby, a tall, red-haired fellow, older than me, sniggered. I tried not to pay him any mind.

"I bet you she shoots better'n you do," John said hotly.

"That's a laugh." Red began to *har-har-har* real loud. He had fat cheeks like a chipmunk. I sure didn't like him.

"We'll see who's laughing."

"John," I whispered, "one more word and I'm going straight home."

Wouldn't you know. They gave me number 13.

Same rules for all.

The others were all pretty good shots. It was exciting to stand there in the crisp autumn air and hold my breath as I watched each one — man or boy — reckon the distance and take heedful aim at his tiny turkey so far away.

When it was the mean fellow's turn, I heard murmuring in the crowd. "Here comes Red." "Crack shot . . ." "Walked off with it last year." "His Pa's been trainin' him since he was knee high."

Red aimed and shot — and he got a bunch of loud hand-clapping. From where I stood, his bullet seemed to fly true, to the head.

I hated that he was such a good shot because he had such a mean mouth.

"Beat that, Petticoat," he muttered.

Best not to answer. I gave John a warning look and just stood, waiting my turn.

"Thirteen," the announcer called, at last.

Walking the few steps ever so slow, I raised my gun and took careful aim. John had come right along with me and stood near me, the fingers of both his hands crossed. Probably his toes were crossed, too, inside his boots, and if he could've worked it, he would've crossed his eyes.

John wanted me to win!

And I wanted to win for him.

I wanted to beat that know-nothing Red.

I squinted through the gun sights, and I saw that small, bright button glinting in the sun far off.

The solitude that always accompanies my taking up a gun to shoot wrapped around me once again. Red, Johnny, all of them were suddenly somewhere else. The world was made up only of that turkey-target and me.

The turkey's glass eye was winking at me.

I pulled the trigger and winked back.

The crowd clapped their hands, and I could hear folks saying, "Didja see what that *girl* did?"

It took a few minutes for the judges to look over all the paper turkeys and compare the shots. Then they voted and the announcer stepped forth.

"Real close decision, folks. Nine had a clean shot to the head, but thirteen whisked the eye clear out." He waved my blinded paper turkey. "Thirteen is a lucky number today. Annie Mozee, the little lady, wins the turkey!"

Now there was clapping for me, loud as thunder. I could feel my face turning red.

"Beginner's luck. Bet you can't do it again," the sore loser said. He had thought the turkey was his.

"Come back next turkey shoot," John answered him, thumbs in his suspenders, hands hanging out and flapping like wings. "You'll see."

We shared the job of lugging home that bird; we had a long ways to go and it was *heavy*!

It was also delicious!

I hoped that Red had to eat chicken for Thanksgiving, a scrawny, tasteless chicken. It would've served him right. Old bread heels in a thin gravy would've been even better.

Well, after that, I began to enter the local shooting matches regular, and I won so often, I finally had to stop.

Folks felt my winning was spoiling it for the other marksmen. I agreed. It's no fun when the same person wins every time.

But winning got me some respect. People knew that Annie Mozee was mighty good with a gun.

And respect was what I wanted most of all.

18

I STOPPED SEWING for hire. Absolutely stopped. I wouldn't stitch anything except clothes for myself or extraspecial things for my family. Designing garments for my kin — drawing the patterns on newspaper and cutting them out — pleased me. Otherwise, I found needlework slow and boring.

"I earn much more money shooting," I told Ma, whenever she tried to coax me back into sewing.

But she didn't give up easy. Not Ma. One day she said, "Thee will accompany me to a sewing meet this afternoon, child. For pleasure."

"Do I have to?"

All the neighbor women would be gathered together, quilting and talking, and their daughters would sit in another place crowded altogether, sewing and giggling. I felt shy.

Ma answered with a frown.

So I went.

There was pleasure.

It was cold cider and a white, frosted layer cake. That was the best part. In fact, that was the only good part.

There were five other girls from neighboring farms,

all hemming and backstitching, sewing up a storm. And they were friendly. Too friendly.

My ordinary sewing was as good as theirs. But I was working on a Sunday dress for Emily, and when they saw my smocking and fagoting stitches they were full of admiration.

They started questioning me and they wouldn't leave off.

"Where did you ever learn to do that, Annie? That's beautiful. How did you learn to stitch so fine?"

Stupid me. I should've brought plain sewing, a muslin petticoat or a red flannel union suit. Their questions terrified me. More than anything I so didn't want them to know I learned fancy sewing at the county poorhouse! I would rather have died than tell them.

"Oops!" I dropped my needle purposely.

Getting down on the floor on my knees to hunt for it, I hoped the conversation would move on to other subjects while I was gone.

As I crept around, I wondered: *How can I get out of this? I can't say Ma taught me the fancy needlework because she is sitting right nearby, and, besides, she doesn't do those stitches.*

"There's your needle," Mary Ames, a pretty yellow-haired girl whose house we were in, called out to me, and she pointed to it helpfully.

Trapped. What could I do?

I picked up the lost needle and raised myself off the floor, dusting off my clothes, and then I faced them all. "I just — sort of — worked the stitches out," I bumbled. "No one really taught me."

"Even if you're very clever," Mary said, "someone must have showed you how."

"I saw sewing pictures in a book," I said desperately. "I just studied them hard and figured out how to do the stitches from them."

I could see by their faces that they didn't believe me, and they thought I was keeping it a secret — maybe out of selfishness. They minded and I felt helpless.

I should have offered to teach them how to do the fancy stitches, but I was too shy. I didn't think of it till later. So I didn't make any friends.

Anyway, their talk did turn to other things, to bread-baking hints and gardening plans and pretty garments they hoped to sew.

I was sorry.

They were nice enough girls, but I couldn't — I *couldn't* — tell them the truth.

"Did thee have a good time?" Ma asked afterward, when we were riding home in the wagon.

"It was all right."

She looked at me close. She sensed that I was unhappy, I guess, because she never insisted that I go again. Not that she gave up. Oh no, that wasn't Ma's way. She'd invite me sure enough whenever she was going to sew and socialize, but I always said no thank you, and she didn't press me.

We went along that way for some time, living peaceably and quietly in North Star.

Till the day Grandpap carried home a fine-looking letter addressed directly to me.

It was written on elegant, stiff, cream-colored paper without any lines, but the handwriting was straight as straight could be.

My sister Lydia and her husband Joe Stein, who lived in Cincinnati, the Queen City of the West, were writing to invite *me* to come and visit!

Ma and I, together, read the invitation out loud; we read it twice. Then I went over it myself word by word.

They were eager for me to come.

"We must send back a no thank you," I decided at once, putting down the invitation.

I was frightened by the memories it brought back of when I'd been away before. I was shaken up by the idea of having to leave North Star. Homesickness had been a fierce ache in me, day and night, those years I was away.

"Consider it," Ma said. "Thee art too hasty."

"I just want to stay here."

"I think thee should go — much as we shall miss thee — and the income," she said gently. "It is a chance to see a grand city, to mix with new people, and to learn many things."

"But I would miss you all — and this place, my home. I feel safe here."

"Home will always be here," she reasoned. "And thee will be safe with Lydia."

"I'd rather not . . . ," I began, but then I saw she wasn't listening.

Her eyes had a faraway, dreamy look. "I came away. I chose to marry Jacob Moses and move west. It is right and proper for a young lady to have choices. Think on it. Thee must decide."

Grandpap was all for me to go. "Cincinnati is a fine city," he argued. "Great wide streets, horsecars, houses big as palaces, and steamboats on the Ohio River. Annie, there's the grand Bevis House Hotel where Mr. John Frost has been servin' your game birds."

He made it sound very tempting as he kept talking.

Still, I was uncertain. "If I go, may I come back whenever I want to?"

"Of course," Ma said. "What a question!"

"You won't want to come back," Grandpap said, shaking his head like he really knew.

"Maybe I could go for a short visit." I was really unsure. "Just to have a look, and see Lydia and meet Joe."

Now Ma was pleased.

"We'll need to make thee some fine new clothes. Two or three dresses and a skirt and several petticoats." Ever practical, she immediately headed for her sewing basket. "I have this special sky-blue lawn put away that would make a lovely frock. It's almost as if I'd known . . ."

The cloth was soft and lovely. Holding it draped

over my shoulder, she let it fall down front in loose folds. She stood behind me, and I could see her face in the mirror. She liked what she saw. "It's becoming."

"You look like a queen, Annie," Emily said.

"Queen of the market hunters." I laughed. "Listen, Ma, I'll only go if I can carry along Pa's gun."

The cloth slipped from her fingers. "Heavens, child. Why?"

"Because when I was alone and helpless, I promised myself I would never be separated from it again. I won't shoot anything in Cincinnati, but I won't go without it."

In Ma's eyes I could see the shadow of the memory of me, starved and bruised, the night I returned from the wolves.

Saddened, she agreed. "Those people did thee great damage."

So it was decided. I was going to Cincinnati, and everyone in our house was excited, me most of all.

I was also the most scared.

Because I realized what this trip meant.

It meant that I was fast growing up!

19

"I THINK I WANT to go back home," were my first words to Lydia, as I stepped off the train and grabbed her. I held on real tight. I'd hardly recognized her in the crowd, in her turquoise city frock with her brown hair all pinned up. "This train station is bigger than all of North Star Village!"

Cincinnati was huge — and loud and packed with people everywhere I looked. Instead of roads in some places there were funny little canals, and they were crowded with boats pulled by mule teams. There seemed to be miles and miles of splendid buildings, and the regular roads were all dangerous to cross because of clanking horsecars.

I'd thought Greenville was a busy place, but Grandpap was right. Cincinnati was amazing.

"Most any place is bigger than North Star," Lydia said, laughing at me. "Don't be silly." She hugged me back. "We're so glad you're here, Annie. Aren't we, Joe?" And then her husband, a great tall man with a homely face — very red as if chilled by winter (but this was only August) — shook my hand and said yes, they were very glad, indeed.

"You'll soon be used to the city," Lydia promised.

"It beats going barefoot and hunting in the woods and the swamp."

"I like going barefoot. I like hunting in the woods and the swamp."

"Annie," Lydia said gravely, "you're fifteen. Almost grown. Give the city a chance. We're going to make you a lady."

"Lydia says you're a great one with a gun." Joe seemed rather shy about mentioning it.

"Joe —" My sister's voice was just like Ma's, calm and quiet but reproving. "That's behind Annie now she's here."

"Look." I pointed to the odd-shaped bundle wrapped in a blanket with my luggage. "I carried my gun along."

"You *what*?" Lydia was properly horrified.

"I had such a hard time without it, Lydia. In the infirmary and then with that evil family. So now I take it wherever I go. Don't worry. I don't guess I'll be hunting anything in Cincinnati."

"I should hope not."

But knowing that my gun was right there with me, Joe wouldn't be stopped. "Why not? There's plenty of shooting in the city, too."

"Shooting?" That surprised me. "At what? Do you hunt your neighbors' cats and dogs?"

He smiled. "No hunting. Mostly target."

My turn to smile. "I did some of that till folks asked me to quit. I was winning too much and spoiling their fun."

"That doesn't sound fair."

"I didn't mind, Joe. I was a market hunter so's our family could live. That's the only reason I ever picked up a gun — and disobeyed my ma with my stubbornness.

"But I do think good hunting is exciting. I mean going after prairie targets — real targets that can run or fly."

"Shooting's a great skill," Joe said. "I was looking forward to seeing you handle a gun." He took my baggage. "I'd be real disappointed if you didn't. You've got to show me — at least one time while you're here. Lyddie?"

"All right. Maybe once," she grudgingly agreed. Then we headed for their home in Fairmount, a pleasant neighborhood.

Cincinnati ran on and on with endless neighborhoods: the riverfront, the stockyards, Germantown with its restaurants and beer halls and music. Lydia and Joe and I spent a lot of the next three months walking; we covered most of the city.

One afternoon we were wandering around in the northern part of town — Joe's favorite area — high up where we could see most of the city sprawling below us. Up there on the heights, amid the beer gardens and restaurants and pavilions, there were shooting galleries and the German Shooting Club.

Joe pointed out the different distant suburbs below, naming them: Hyde Park; Mill Creek; Fairmount, where we lived; and Oakley. "Some of them were separate small towns once," Joe said, "then they got swept into being part of the city."

I looked toward Oakley fondly, remembering the Reverend Sylvester.

"What do you say we try a little shooting?" Joe suggested. When my sister looked unhappy, he reminded her, "You promised, Lyddie."

I showed my empty palms. "I haven't my gun."

"Not needed." He led me into Charlie Stuttelberg's Shooting Gallery. There were metal targets — ducks and rabbits — traveling along on a mechanical track.

"Hello, Charlie. Want you to meet my family." Joe introduced us to the man in the shirtsleeves sitting to one side reading a German newspaper.

"Watch," Joe said to me, picking up one of the gallery's guns. He aimed and shot six times, but only two tin ducks went down, each accompanied by a clanging bell. Nary a rabbit fell. "I'm rusty," he said, disgusted. "I usually do better than that. Your turn, Annie." He pointed to a gun.

"What do I get if I shoot true?"

Mr. Stuttelberg looked up from his newspaper and made a noise deep in his throat. It wasn't a laugh, but it was first cousin to one.

"Five out of six and you don't pay."

I took careful aim. It was an unfamiliar gun, but this kind of shooting was so easy it was a joke.

Three shots, three tin ducks down, three bells!

Three more shots, three tin rabbits down, three more bells!

Setting down the gun gently, I dusted off my hands.

Mr. Stuttelberg folded up his newspaper and unfolded himself out of the chair. "Where'd you learn to shoot like that?"

"Out in the country."

"She's a market hunter. Been selling her quail to John Frost for a long time now," Joe boasted.

"*You're* the one? John Frost is in my shooting club. He's told me about the birds you send. Shoot again, young lady," Charlie Stuttelberg said. "You won a free round."

"Uh-uh," Lydia objected. "No more. We have an agreement."

"Please, I have to see her do that again. Very few ever walk in here off the street cold and knock down six in a row. No woman ever has, not in the thirteen years I've had this gallery."

There was that number 13.

Well, I picked up a fresh gun and did it again.

And again.

Even Lydia was amazed.

"How'd you like to be part of the Thanksgiving Day shooting matches I run for the club," Mr. Stuttelberg invited, "on Schuetzenbuckle?"

"Shooter's Hill," Joe translated.

"Annie . . . ," Lydia warned softly.

"Sorry, Mr. Stuttelberg. I promised my sister no more shooting. Just this once."

"There's a crack shot performing on the stage in the theaters here," Mr. Stuttelberg said, addressing himself particularly to Lydia. "Frank Butler. Part of the team Butler and Graham?"

She really didn't want to hear about it, so she shook her head, but he was strong willed.

"This here Frank Butler is an incredible shot. Shoots little crystal balls tossed up in the air. Shoots playing cards. Can shoot a coin out of his partner's hand."

"Good-natured fellow, he likes to challenge the locals. Always wins. I've lost a pile of money betting against him, but I believe this young lady could take him. On behalf of the club, I'm willing to put a fifty-dollar purse on her at the Thanksgiving meet."

"Fifty dollars!" I gasped. "In Darke County, I won a Thanksgiving shoot and got a *turkey*. Beat a bully named Red, who was pretty good, but I was just a whit better."

The idea of shooting against a showman who could do marvelous tricks was exciting.

"It'd be trapshooting with pigeons."

I hesitated. "I never did that."

"It's a breeze, Annie," Joe assured me.

"I'll do all the arranging," Charlie Stuttelberg went on. "All you need to do is say yes. You win, you keep the purse."

I was shaking my head, refusing. I'd promised Lydia, and a promise was a promise.

"First woman in a shooting match on the hill," Mr. Stuttelberg chuckled. "I can't wait to see Butler's face when he loses."

We all looked to Lydia, but she was silent.

"I'll up it to *one hundred* dollars." Mr. Stuttelberg was really tickled by the idea.

He could see we were stunned by the amount. "We'll make it back in bets," he said. "No problem at all."

"Lydia, you've got to let her," Joe argued. "Annie's something special. She'll win it sure." He was just glowing with pride.

"Well, Joe," I said, "thanks, but I don't know about that *sure*. I would like a chance against this fancy marksman."

The three of us all arguing for the shooting match were so excited, we wore Lydia down. She tried her best, but she couldn't hold out.

"All right," she finally agreed. "But just this one Thanksgiving Day match. One more shoot can't matter too much, I guess. After that, you'll just pack up that gun forever, Annie; hear?"

Dear Lydia. Nobody ever guessed more wrong.

20

THAT NOVEMBER OF 1875 was unseasonably warm, so on Thanksgiving Day we didn't need coats. On Shooter's Hill crowds wearing their best finery wandered through the park to watch about a hundred different shooting matches.

And to eat and drink and celebrate.

Weaving back and forth through the crowds were salesmen in white aprons calling their wares: "Herring! Strudel! Pretzels! Beer! Cigars!" They moved about, jingling the coins in their apron pockets as they served.

People stood around or sat on benches, talking and laughing while they enjoyed their food and beer. It was very festive.

Joe treated us to strudel, squares of raisin applecake layered in paper-thin dough, and sweet lemonade that reminded me of the Bunburys.

Joe insisted on carrying my gun and the other equipment. I would have argued, but Lydia looked so fashionable and ladylike in her fine gray dress and bonnet, that me marching alongside her with a long-barreled cap-and-ball Pennsylvania rifle slung on my shoulder would've spoiled the effect.

I was dressed up, too, in the sky-blue frock Ma had sewed for me, and my hair was tied back with a matching satin ribbon. Lydia cut me short, frizzy bangs for my forehead. The frizzles looked cute.

We followed Joe to the shooting field, edging our way through the jostling mob.

Something odd about the city, I noted: people got all dressed up to shoot here. Many of the men were wearing real fancy belted shooting coats.

I thought fondly of my hunting outfit back home, a coffee sack pulled over my linsey dress, Pa's old cap, and the too-big boots, and I smiled to myself. What did it matter what a marksman wore? What mattered was talent!

Yet, I was glad Ma had sewed me this two-piece blue dress of soft lawn, the skirt with a tight waist, and the bodice loose with wide sleeves and square wood buttons to the waist. My arms were free to move up high, to raise a gun. This dress was almost Ma's permission. I liked to think so.

Groundsmen were raking up the area, cleaning away dead birds, and drawing a fresh new target line. At the table, Joe stopped and handed over my rifle and other stuff, saying, "Set your gear out, Annie. Make yourself comfortable. And good luck."

I began to lay the various items out: my powder horn, shot pouch, ramrod — the works. "Who am I shooting against, Joe?"

Joe hunched his shoulders to show he didn't know. Then he turned, squinting in the bright sunlight, and he scanned the crowd spread out over the field. "Wait." He pointed over to the left. "Here comes Charlie Stuttelberg. Take a look at the fellow with him, the one wearing the shooting coat with medals on his chest."

I did my best to look without directly staring. A tall, handsome man with a mustache walked alongside Charlie, nodding and smiling as they talked.

"The one wearing the soft green hat with the feather?"

"Chances are that's him," Joe guessed.

Suddenly I felt real nervous. I wished I was any place but right there. I turned my attention to my gun, which I was dusting off with a cloth.

Soon, a voice from behind us called, "Hello, Joe, Annie."

Then Charlie was saying, "Frank, I'd like to introduce you to your opponent. This young lady is Annie Mozee. Annie, turn around and meet the fellow you're going to clobber, Frank Butler."

Blushing, I turned around. He couldn't hide the surprise on his face. He'd thought all along it was Joe he was matched against. Charlie hadn't told him I was a girl.

That's what I'll always remember about the first glance we exchanged. Frank Butler didn't even blink. He had honest blue eyes. He looked directly at me and he smiled, cool, like he had known what was coming all the while. "Pleased to meet you, Miss Mozee," he said, taking off his hat.

"I guess Charlie didn't tell you I was a girl."

"No." He was still amused. "He left that little fact out of the picture."

"Does it matter?"

"Naah. That's probably why he didn't bother to mention it."

That made me grin. "Wouldn't bet on it."

He grinned right along with me. He understood exactly.

The signal went off in my mind: *Bang!* This is a true friend.

I knew from that very first minute that Frank Butler was a good, fair man.

"You must be something special to get old Charlie to put up such a purse," he teased.

I didn't know what to say or where to look. Luckily, just then the announcer called, "Butler, Mozee," and the crowd surged our way.

All around us there was excited, rowdy money talk. People were betting wildly, mostly on him.

Except for Charlie and my brother-in-law Joe. Bless him. Joe was betting all he had, and some he didn't have, on me.

Lydia just stood to a side, pale and a bit frightened-looking.

"Time," the referee called.

We went to the shooting station and listened while he bawled out the rules. Two traps. Distance: twenty yards. Twenty-five birds apiece. Guns kept below the elbow till the call, "Pull."

Frank Butler was using a single-shot Winchester. I had faith in my old muzzle-loader.

I could feel my face wet with perspiration. Oh, how I wished my brother Johnny were standing there near me, as he usually was, with his fingers and toes crossed.

All of this — the place, the crowds, the betting, the traps — was so unfamiliar. I longed for home.

There was no time for that.

The coin toss. Frank Butler won, so he had the first turn.

We moved to our places.

"Are you both ready?" the referee boomed.

"Yes," we answered.

I watched carefully, studying every single detail: Frank's posture, his hands, the angle of his feet — everything.

"Pull," he called.

Behind the mound the trap sprung open with a loud clang.

The gun swung to his shoulder just as the pigeon sailed high through the air. Frank's eye stayed with the bird.

He fired.

"Hit!" the referee called.

The crowd was generous with its cheers, then it became strangely quiet.

They just didn't know what to make of me. I could hear whispers, questions: "Who is she?" "Someone from up-country?" "Must be or she'd know better'n to

challenge Butler." "I heard she's a crack shot."
"G'wan. He'll wipe her out." "He's a pro." "I saw him
on the stage at the Coliseum riddling playing cards full
of holes."

My turn.

All the eyes were looking to me. His eyes, too.

Frank Butler's blue blue eyes.

I was scared. I'd overreached myself. I wasn't usually a showoff, but Cincinnati and all my brother-in-
law's praises, as well as Charlie Stuttelberg's, had
turned my head and made me do this fool thing.

I looked to Lydia. Citified, ladylike Lydia had for-
gotten herself; she had both hands swung up high,
fingers crossed, and she was chanting silently our old
cry from back home, "Pigeon ho! Pigeon ho!" like I
had already downed the bird. I had to smile and that
heartened me.

My gun was ready. I closed my eyes for a second
and pictured myself back in the woods at home, watching a covey of quail rise out of the bush. I had to
recollect the motion exactly, so that I would move up
with my target's grace and when it was in place I
would fire.

I wet my lips with the tip of my tongue.

Avis, I heard Johnny's happy whispered warning.

"Pull," I called, and with that the pigeon rose, and
my gun right along with it.

And I fired

My eye had truly followed the arc of the bird. I'd
dropped him on the rise within the boundary line.

I'd done it!

Joy replaced the fear within me.

Confirmation came with the call. "Hit!"

The pigeon plummeted to the earth.

The crowd applauded. I looked to my opponent. He looked thoughtful and tipped his hat gallantly.

Oh well, it was only the first shot. He could afford to be generous.

He didn't have much to do between shots. He just had to snap his sleek rifle open at the breech, put a bullet in, then snap it shut.

I had to hustle: cleaning, measuring, ramming. But I wouldn't have traded Pa's old gun for anything.

Well, we began to down the birds, and a regular rhythm developed.

Ooh! said the crowd at each shot. *Aah!* they exclaimed as the bird fell.

And each time, he'd look to me and then I back to him and there was no anger, only interest between us, appreciation and admiration of fine shooting. It was a queer afternoon.

He missed his fifteenth shot, but I missed my eighteenth, so by nineteen we were tied again and we stayed that way through twenty-four.

His turn.

Joe, my brother-in-law, was about to explode. He was all red-faced and perspiring, jumping up and down when he wasn't pacing. Lydia had to go stand beside him and put her hands on his big shoulders and press him down like a jack-in-the-box.

"Folks," the referee called, and then he had to wait because the crowd was so noisy with its excitement. "Now, folks, we need you to quiet down, please. Match point here."

Frank Butler readied himself.

"Pull," he called for that last bird.

The pigeon rose up, quartering to the right, and his shot came just a hair's breadth too late. The bullet grazed the bird's tail feathers, but off it flew.

"Miss," came the call.

Ooh! moaned the crowd.

Then they hushed up without anyone needing to tell them to.

Every eye was on me as I moved forward, oddly calm and ready now. It was as if I'd used up all my nervousness, all my fears and doubts.

I looked to Frank Butler. He seemed calm and very interested.

"Pull," I called, and then I heard the trap door's noise and saw my bird. My gun was in place, my cheek firm against the woodstock. I saw that my bird, also, was oddly twisting away up high. I corrected the angle till my eye saw true.

I fired.

"Hit!" came the referee's call.

"*Aaaah!*" said the crowd.

There was tumult all around me. Joe was dancing, dancing around and around with Lydia.

Our scores were announced and there was cheering. Charlie Stuttelberg came hurrying over to hand me a small soft purse with metal clasps. "Well-earned," he said. "I don't know when I've enjoyed a match so much."

I turned over my winnings to Lydia for safekeeping and headed toward the loading table to collect my gear.

Frank Butler was there, waiting.

"Good shooting," he said, offering his hand.

"For a girl?" I don't know why I was mean-mouthed when he was so generous. Embarrassment maybe. I was immediately sorry. But he didn't take offense.

"For anyone," he said.

"You're awful good yourself. I hear you do trick shooting in an act on the stage."

"Yes," he said. "We're on a tour. We leave tomorrow for Pittsburgh —"

Just then Charlie Stuttelberg came over to us. "Come, folks," he said. "I'm buying dinner for my friends."

"The loser, too?" Frank wondered.

"The loser especially." Charlie slapped him on the shoulder. "Because this little lady has made him a poorer man today."

"I'm sorry," I murmured.

"No, you're not," Frank said, laughing.

"You're right. I'm really not."

"Come along," Charlie said. "You both have earned your dinners."

21

IN THE HEIDELBERG BEER GARDEN, a brass band was playing and people were dancing and eating and talking. Waiters hurried about, balancing loaded trays above their heads.

"We can have our dinner outdoors if you like," Frank suggested. "That way we can talk."

"I'd like that," I said.

He made the explanations to the others: We needed a little quiet after the shooting match to calm ourselves down. Especially me because I was only a very young girl.

I did my best not to giggle. I was pretty calm.

So we two sat outside on the grass terrace amid the blooming red rose bushes at a small table covered by a white cloth and lit by a candle.

"Roast goose and red cabbage?" Frank suggested. "It's their specialty."

"Mmm," I agreed.

He ordered, and then we talked a blue streak till the food came and all the while we ate.

He began by making me feel comfortable.

"I like to talk," he said, "when I've got the right audience. You seem like the right audience."

"I like to listen."

He had much to tell. He was twenty-five, ten years older'n me, and he'd set out from Ireland, all alone, when he was thirteen years old, working for his passage aboard ship.

"Why?" I asked. "Weren't you scared? What made you go?"

"My folks were dead," he said simply. "You wouldn't believe how terrible things were back home. Da had farmed for British landlords — potatoes were the main crop — and when the crops failed, farmers were evicted."

The memories made him sad. "There was famine. My family wandered the roads with thousands of other ragged, starving, beggars. That's the life I ran away from."

I wanted to take his hand and hold it to comfort him. But of course I didn't. Instead, I said, "You were brave."

"I don't know about brave. When you have no choice, you do what you can."

I understood that very well. *Stubborn* is what Ma called it. *Unseemly.* But I had no choice, same as Frank.

"In New York I found work, but not exactly high-falutin jobs." He grinned. "I drove a milk wagon, I was a stable boy, I sold newspapers, and then for a long time I worked on a fishing boat."

"What brought you to shooting?"

"I needed a better life, so I looked around. Seeing animal acts in vaudeville gave me an idea. I'm good with dogs, so I bought a couple of smart animals and trained them to do tricks: tumble and jump and dance on their hind legs. We got some theater bookings. Then I decided to learn sharpshooting. And that practically brings me up to date.

"But I've gone on much too long about myself —"

"No," I protested. "Not a bit. The shooting really interests me."

"Well, I practiced till my hands were numb and my eyes bleary. But I got good at it and learned to love it. Then I teamed up with John Graham. We get plenty of bookings east of the Mississippi — like the Coliseum here."

He stopped. "And now, Annie, it's your turn. Tell me how you happened to become such a good shot that it cost me Charlie Stuttelberg's hundred-dollar purse."

I began way back with Pa's dying and all that had happened to me.

"Mmm," he'd say every so often. Just, "Mmm," softly.

When I got up to Mary Jane dying, he reached over and took my hand and held it, and I felt safe.

I wasn't even ashamed to tell about the county home and Emmeline Sue Smathers and the wolves. I'd never talked about them since the night I came back home to Ma, but somehow it seemed natural that Frank would understand.

I told him about my running away and meeting the Bunburys and lying to them so they'd get me on the train. I told him everything there was to tell about me.

He just sat there and listened, and when I was done he was quiet awhile.

Then he said, "I'm real sorry I have to go away tomorrow, Annie. We'll be touring till next summer. Then I'd like to come back to see you. Will you still be here?"

"Here or not very far away. Maybe back home in North Star. I'm going to spend some time studying and reading and writing. And, of course, practicing my shooting."

"Whoa!" he said, drawing back like he was scared. "There's no need for that. You're already a first-rate shot."

"You can't ever be too good," I said. "You know that."

Just then Lydia came out the door looking for us. "Come on, you two," she called. "You're wanted inside."

We rose and followed her back in, Frank holding on to my hand.

When we got to the big round table where my family and friends were celebrating, Charlie Stuttelberg stood up and tapped his mug with a spoon till he got some quiet. Then he raised the brimming glass. "Ladies and gentlemen," he said, "I would like to offer a toast: To a little lady who's a crackerjack shot. To Annie —"

They all rose and lifted their glasses high and said it together right after him. "To Annie —"

"— a shooting star!" he finished, and he drank.

Folks sipped then applauded.

I curtsied first to the right, then to the left.

"Ma would admire the way you curtsied," Lydia whispered to me. "You're a regular lady." I squeezed her hand to say thanks for that.

When I peeked over at Frank Butler, he was looking proud and ever so happy for me.

I mean — he *had* lost the hundred-dollar purse!

Right then I thought of Pa and his fairy tales.

In them the lovely young maiden and the handsome prince just glance at one another and *know* they were meant for each other.

I always marveled at those stories.

Till it happened to me.

Love at first sight at a big, rowdy shooting match — where the maiden beat the prince.

22

THAT WAS WHEN MY GIRLHOOD actually ended. I was fifteen years old when Frank went off on his theater tour. I returned to North Star to wait for him and practice my shooting.

And that was when I intended my story to end.

But I need to tidy things up a bit.

And there is one truly remarkable event I have to tell about . . .

Frank came back before the end of the year, and we were married — that *was* remarkable, but it wasn't the "event!"

After we were married, we formed a vaudeville team, Butler and Butler, traveling across the country performing in theaters, doing what we loved best — sharpshooting.

Till the agents said they weren't using "family acts" like Butler and Butler anymore.

So I had to change my name.

Recollecting that my dear friend the Reverend Sylvester Bunbury had called me *Annie Oakley* during my train ride to freedom, I took that name for good.

I became so skilled at trick shooting, Frank decided to stop performing in order to assist and manage me.

Our act, Oakley and Butler, was mighty popular.
We worked together beautifully.

He tossed up crystal balls and I blasted them in midair.

With a gun on my shoulder pointed backward, I looked in a mirror and fired, hitting targets he held up behind me.

Each time he displayed a playing card, I riddled it as full of holes as a slice of Swiss cheese.

I shot coins out of his hands.

I shot the ash from a cigarette in his mouth!

And sometimes we did a specialty number with a member of the audience.

So — one night in Louisville, Kentucky, after our regular routine, I stepped forward on the stage. "Can we have a volunteer with a steady hand to come up and help us?" I asked.

There was the usual murmur and laughter as people urged their *friends* to volunteer, but no one rose.

"Come on, folks," I coaxed. "Surely there's one critter here who trusts Annie Oakley."

The one person in the world who shouldn't have stood up.

A young *woman* in the balcony shouted, "Hey, Sharpshooter. I'm not afraid."

I'd heard that voice before, somewhere. Long ago.

"Come right ahead," I invited. Frank and I had done this act a hundred times and never — *never* — before had a woman volunteered.

Frank wiped the surprised look off his face and took

center stage to entertain the crowd while she made her way to the front.

I waited in the wings.

Once we were face-to-face, I made the connection.

Yellow hair, not tangled now but nicely done up in a bun. More freckles than a trout.

A haunt from the worst time in my life.

"Minute you stepped out, I knew it was you," she said, looking me over close.

She must've been eating good these past years because she was large. Two chins and a big bottom. She was stuffed into a terrible, tight, green store-bought dress, covered with bright pink cabbage roses, the kind of pattern that belongs on upholstery. She resembled an upright sofa.

"Emmeline Sue —" I said.

She grinned.

"— I heard you burned the farmer's springhouse down."

Her eyes glittered with pleasure. "He deserved it."

"I agree with you. I also heard you ran off with two hundred dollars?" I looked at her inquiringly.

"That's more'n you got." Her smile was sly. "You think I took it?"

I was glad she rattled right on talking, so I didn't have to answer that question.

"I have a good life here. I work as a cook, and I bought a share of a restaurant. I got me a boyfriend — Beauregard. He's right up there lookin' at us," she boasted, ever so pleased with herself. She kept on going.

"I told Beau I knew you once. He laughed and double-dared me to come down. He'd sure love for you to say hello to him."

Now she was proud to know me. *Now* she was using me to show off.

"Emmeline Sue, you were so mean to me back in the infirmary you sure you want to do this? Aren't you scared I'll shoot you in the heart — accidentally?"

"Naah! You wouldn't. Like you couldn't that night back in the poorhouse."

"I didn't have a gun then. I was bluffing."

She shrugged.

Ma was right; Emmeline Sue was not likable. In fact, she was absolutely hateable. But she had courage.

For a minute there, I almost admired her.

Which was a terrible mistake. The trout doesn't change its spots.

Because the next thing she did was to bend over and pinch the soft leather of my skirt. "Say, ain't you something." Her tone was envious. She held her opened hand to one side of her mouth and recited into my ear:

> Moses-Poses
> Moses-Poses
> Where'd you get
> the fancy clothes-es . . . ?

Same rotten old Emmeline Sue Smathers.

"I'm not going to use you in the act," I said calmly. "I'm going to announce to the crowd that you were too scared."

"No!" she said, dismayed. "You can't do that."

"Sure I can. It's happened before. People are brave in their seats, then they come up here and get chick-enhearted. You can just march right back up to that balcony —"

"Beau will laugh at me. I didn't mean nothin'. Can'tcha take a joke?"

"Nope."

"I take it back," she pleaded. "I take it back double."

"This is not the infirmary, and we're not kids. You can't take it back."

"I'll never do it again," she swore. "I'll never say your name again so long as I live." And then she actually began to blubber. Emmeline Sue Smathers! Cryin'.

I didn't say a word.

"Please, you'll spoil my life," she begged. "Please."

That time on the stage in Louisville was probably the only time she'd said *please* in her whole life. It shouldn't have got to me, but it did. I could have destroyed her.

Out front the audience was getting restless.

Now Frank was introducing us. "Ladies and gentle-man, pay close attention as Annie Oakley shoots holes in the queen of spades, held by . . . your name, brave lady?"

"Emmeline Sue Smathers."

He recognized her name and was startled.

"It's all right, Frank," I murmured.

Placing the card between her fingers, he stationed her carefully, showing her exactly where to stand and how to extend her arm. "Don't move a hair's breadth," he warned.

"You don't need to tell *me*," she said.

I took my time looking over the gun, checking everything. The rustling in the audience showed the crowd was anxious. Slowly the whole house grew quiet. I could hear Emmeline Sue's breathing, shallow and quick. She wasn't quite as calm as she made out.

I lifted the gun and took aim.

I fired a series of shots.

The card was riddled with holes.

"The lady gets to keep the card!" Frank announced. "She can use it for a colander." Folks laughed at that.

Usually I shook hands with the volunteer, but I didn't feel like it. I did step up to the footlights and look up at the balcony. "Hey, Beau," I called. "The one thing your girl's got is guts!" To her I murmured, "Remember your promise."

"I owe you, Annie," she whispered, as we took our bows — *the first and only time she ever spoke my name right!* — and, clutching the card, she hurried off into the darkened theater.

As I write this, I still have not forgiven her.

I'm not sorry she burned the springhouse down.

I'll never know if she took the farmer's money.

Nor will I know if she kept her word about my name.

I guess I'm glad she made herself a life.

Everyone is entitled to a life!

Even Emmeline Sue Smathers.

After she went, I stood watching the theater empty, and suddenly I felt terribly, terribly weary. The meeting with Emmeline Sue had been too much. All those poor wretched infirmary orphans marched through my mind. Along with the old farm woman who kept saying, "Porridge and pork chops, porridge and pork chops," all day long.

Shivering now, I was transported back to the poor farm, to the bitter cold and the hard work and the foul smells, all of us shut up indoors, sewing, sewing, sewing.

And Mrs. Eddington telling me my future: "Sewing is a useful and respectable trade. You will make an excellent seamstress one day."

And then came the wolves . . .

I stood there frozen till Frank came onto the darkened stage looking for me. He took my hand. "Annie," he said, "we've got a surprise visitor backstage. Buffalo Bill Cody —"

"You're kidding."

"No. He was in the audience, and he's come to speak the sweetest words you ever heard."

The look of awe on Frank's face was enough to send me skedaddling backstage, tired as I was.

And they were sweet words. He invited Frank and me to join his Wild West Show. He particularly wanted a woman sharpshooter.

Of course I said yes.

Author's Note

This story is based on the real life of the clever, brave, very gifted Annie Oakley. All of the major events in the book are true.

She did get sent to the poorhouse where she was cruelly teased about her name; she did live with Mr. and Mrs. wolf; she did run away to escape from their bondage, and a stranger did pay her train fare; she did win the Shooter's Hill match in Cincinnati and marry Frank Butler before she was sixteen.

And she did join Buffalo Bill's Wild West Show and go on to become the best and most famous international sharpshooter.

Emmeline Sue Smathers, Sally Jones, and the Bunburys are my creations. Most of the rest of the folks in this book really lived, but of course the one who lived, and lives, most vividly is the remarkable Annie Oakley.

Bibliography

Rogers, Will. *The Autobiography of Will Rogers.* Edited by Donald Day. Boston: Houghton Mifflin, 1926.

Havighurst, Walter. *Annie Oakley of the Wild West.* New York: MacMillan, 1954.

Holbrook, Stewart. *Little Annie Oakley and Other Rugged People.* New York: MacMillan, 1948.

Kasper, Shirl. *Annie Oakley.* Norman: University of Oklahoma Press, 1992.

Levine, Ellen. *Ready, Aim, Fire: The Real Adventures of Annie Oakley.* New York: Scholastic, Inc., 1989.

Swartout, Annie Fern. *Missie: The Life and Times of Annie Oakley.* Blanchester, Ohio: Brown Publishing, 1947.